The One

MARGOT SWIFT

COPYRIGHT © 2019 MARGOT SWIFT

DISCLAIMER

All characters in this book are purely fictional with no reference to any living person.

References to hotels and public houses are fictional and have no reference to any business or premise that may contain the same business name or type of business.

CONTENTS

Chapter 1 That Day

You know those dark, damp November mornings where the cold penetrates your bones and the world looks like it's coming to an end? Well this was one of those mornings in rural Lincolnshire. On mornings such as these it often seems that the only sensible thing to do is to stay indoors, drink a hot cup of tea and monitor the world outside from within, preferably in close proximity to a blazing log fire.

On this certain day, staying at home wasn't an option for Cam, he had arranged to meet an old colleague, Neil, for a coffee. Since their retirement from police service they met infrequently, however, on this occasion Neil apparently had some very important news to disclose. Meeting Neil itself was a pleasure but the meeting was in London. Cam's dislike of the hustle and bustle, noise and grime of cities was deep and longstanding. His dislike was born from his time working there as a serving police officer. He was raised in rural Lincolnshire and was a country boy at heart.

Cam woke, as he does most mornings at 6.30, and followed his usual routine. He got his much loved log burner going followed by walking his 12-year-old faithful German Shepherd dog, Colin. An unusual name for a dog but it suited his calm, reliable nature. During some tough times that Cam had suffered, Colin appeared to be his only ally and friend. In this case it's certainly true what they say about being a man's best friend. Cam, as ever, thoroughly enjoyed his walk with Colin, he adored the moments of peace and tranquility he found within the many acres of arable farmland that surrounded his home. However, this particular morning was different, Cam felt an uneasiness in himself, as though something was about to happen that was beyond his control.

Upon returning home he decided to eat breakfast prior to his journey - he was reluctant to pay overinflated city prices for food. He opened the cupboard with the intention of choosing some cereal but as the cupboards were almost bare, he wasn't burdened by the choice. After eating the toasted stale bread, Cam decided to warm himself in front of the log burner, it was a battle between himself and Colin as to who could get the most salubrious spot. Colin, with a little persuasion, moved across slightly in order that Cam could make the most of the heat.

Sufficiently warmed, and after long deliberation as to whether he should actually make the effort to travel to the city or not, he unenthusiastically dragged himself away from the log burner and made his way to the bathroom. He was like a child being forced to go to school, when all the child wanted to do was stay at home.

The journey was a short one as his home was a small, one-bedroom, bungalow which was once a tied property to a farm, hence the acres of farmland that it stood within. It was the ideal property for Cam due to his lack of affinity with people, and because he felt that the world was frenzied, fake, and without moral. His opinion of society in general was that people were greedy and self-obsessed, living on a treadmill which usually only offered focus on the unobtainable carrot, wealth and happiness, which subsequently obliterated any chance of them seeing the beautiful things in life. This was not an inherited view but one that had formed due to his experience of life.

In the bathroom he looked in the mirror, deciding whether he should bother to shave or not. Looking back at him he saw a man who was in his mid-fifties with a face which had a story to tell; although still ruggedly handsome, blue eyes, greying hair in need of a trim and his own teeth. He gave the impression that he had no real interest in his appearance. His profession, together with the events of an uneasy and stressful life, had certainly not left him unscathed. He decided, predictably, that the visit to the city was not a worthwhile reason for the inconvenience of shaving.

As he looked into the reflection of his eyes he saw a man who lacked zest and ambition, a man hiding a deep sadness and going through the motions of existing, not truly living but just existing. Unfortunately for Cam, this was a sight he had grown to accept with the realisation that there was not much he could do, or wanted to do, about it.

His next decision was whether to shower or not. His professional career had a direct influence on this. In many situations he had no alternative other than to put his hands on people, many of those were unwashed, with dirty bodies, clothes and underwear. He remembered the embarrassment and humiliation this had caused some of them, so without hesitation he jumped into the shower. Cam had strong beliefs, which over the years had been questioned and tested, but he had continually put others' welfare first, at times severely neglecting his own.

After a quick shower it was time for him to dress. This task never caused him any problems, he always selected the most comfortable attire he could get away with. In the eyes of others his dress sense, at times, appeared most inappropriate. It had been many years since he had felt the need to or required to dress to impress. The result meant that on this particular day he wore an old T-shirt, which had been accidentally bleach stained and had obviously seen better days, his favourite fleece top which was collarless and a disgusting green in colour, a pair of old jeans and a pair of old walking shoes, which gave the impression of having covered thousands of miles and suffered much abuse. His black duffle coat had been purchased from a charity shop some years earlier. He found great pleasure in shopping in charity shops for two reasons; it saved waste and provided much needed money for good causes. Cam certainly wasn't dressed to impress, but it was his way and he was comfortable.

He placed Colin in the veranda, he left him in there when he knew he was going to be away for a few hours so that Colin could go in and out of the garden at his leisure. As he closed the house door to the veranda he said,

"See you later, Colin. I won't be too long."

Cam then questioned himself as to why he had said this to Colin. Firstly, Colin couldn't understand him, and secondly, if Neil is given the opportunity, he will talk for hours. He knew that Colin was only interested in a comfortable bed and a full stomach, both of which he had. Neil was a good friend, but the older Cam got, the less he became inclined to have needless conversation, even with friends.

Cam closed and locked the front door and prior to getting into his car he checked his post box. He retrieved a couple of letters from within, both were addressed to Mr Cameron Grant, this was his indication of whether his mail was personal or business. As these letters indicated business, he subsequently pushed them unceremoniously into his coat pocket and got into his car.

His car was a true reflection of his own personality. It was a dark blue VW Polo Estate, manufactured in 1989, 1300cc engine with no bells or whistles. It was basic, fit for purpose, reliable, simple enough to do some home mechanics on, inconspicuous and by the majority of people, undervalued. However, Cam could not be quite as predictable as fine German engineering as he had human traits that could not be ignored; emotion and depth of thought, they made him both strong and vulnerable at the same time. Without doubt he had a certain complexity about him.

The VW Polo fired into life at the first turn of the key, as it usually did. As he slowly manoeuvred down the dirt track to the road he looked in his rear view mirror at his bungalow. It wasn't aesthetically pleasing to the eye but it was his much loved home. Every time he left it he looked forward to getting back to the things that it offered which he valued so highly, anonymity together with peace and tranquility.

Decision time again for Cam as he turned on the radio. "What do I fancy today?" he asked himself regarding the choice of music. His music tastes were very much varied, ranging from Led Zeppelin, right through to classical, from pulsating rock beats and acoustic ballads to the haunting sound of the cello. In his youth he had attended many rock concerts to see bands such as AC/DC, Motorhead and at Knebworth in 1979, Led Zeppelin.

Even back then he had a diverse taste in music, he considered himself lucky to have experienced such a wide variety. He adored music that gave him the opportunity to apply his own interpretation to it, thus opening up his mind and soul. He only opened up to himself now though, times of opening up to other people were long behind him. For Cam, being alone was a defence mechanism to avoid upset and disappointment. With this belief he accepted the feeling of being mildly content compared to being truly happy.

Due to the long drive he chose to listen to classical music, the first piece he heard was one of his favourites, 'Dumbledore's Farewell' by Nicholas Hooper. He found this music very deep and moving which allowed his thoughts to explore corners of his mind and heart.

"Not a bad start to the day," he muttered as he turned onto the tarmac road where his journey commenced in earnest.

During his drive to London, he had numerous thoughts about many things, some triggered by the events happening on his journey and others that continually haunted him. The thoughts and feelings that haunted him played a large part in moulding him into the person he had become. Cam had a broken marriage behind him, four grown-up children with ages ranging from 21 to 34, of which two were boys and two were girls. He also had three grandchildren. Due to differences of opinion after his divorce, two of his children had ceased contact with him for two years. His youngest daughter's contact was by text message only, and two very brief and emotional encounters. His eldest son and grandchildren were in regular contact and maintained a good relationship with him. Cam was a young man when he became a father so for the majority of his adult life he had cared for, provided for and raised a family. With everything he had worked for and cared about seemingly in tatters, it was little wonder why he had taken the defensive step to withdraw from the outside world. The hope of reconciliation and optimism, that he once held onto so tightly, was being slowly wrenched from his grasp by the realisation that he was now excess to requirements.

Those events not only took from him his financial security and pride, but raised doubts in his belief in himself. He was adamant that nobody would infiltrate his emotions again, or be in a position to destroy what little optimism, goodwill and fun, that remained. He saw his affection as being similar to a hand that feeds a dog, if it keeps getting bitten, it's inevitable that the hand will protect itself and cease to feed the dog.

More so than most men, Cam tried to hide - and was very successful in doing so - his sadness, turmoil, frustration and at times helplessness. He strongly believed in not burdening others with his problems and if the situation so required, he could provide a false smile and tell the world he was fine. He now saw his life as something to be endured and lived out, opposed to something that should be embraced, cherished and greeted with enthusiasm, something which he used to do.

Cam used his driving skills to good effect during his journey, he made steady progress in all the available places and was very considerate to other road users. He looked after his trusty VW as though it was an old friend, perhaps more so, he certainly adored and respected it. It was never asked to do what it would struggle with, and never mistreated, he very rarely went above 60 mph. During his police career, Cam had (amongst other roles) served as a driving and motorcycle instructor. This enabled him to see hazards and opportunities earlier than most other road users, which made his progress as quick as most other drivers, but without continuous accelerating and braking. However, having this skill also enabled him to recognise bad driving and potential accidents earlier than most, at times this resulted in him becoming frustrated with other drivers and despondent with travel.

As he reached the outskirts of London where the pace of life in comparison to rural Lincolnshire became all too evident, he felt himself retreating further into his shell. He sarcastically said to himself,

"I'm sat in traffic, on a grey day, on a grey street, surrounded by grey buildings. Could it possibly get any worse?"

As soon as he finished saying that he heard an almighty bang. He looked to his left and saw that a cycle courier had caught his door mirror.

"You fucking idiot!!!" he shouted fearing that his beloved VW had suffered damage.

He soon realised that it hadn't and began to calm down a little, it was not needed, but this incident confirmed to Cam that he did not belong in this environment. An apology from the courier would have eased his frustration considerably.

The traffic moved slowly forward offering new views for Cam to gaze into, like a man who has been hypnotised and had every last breath sucked from him. However, he did see something that was either going to make him chuckle with self-righteousness and gratitude that he didn't live there, or feel total despair. A teenage pedestrian with his hood up, potentially due to the consistent drizzle, stepped onto the road to cross it without so much as taking a glance. As a result, a car braked sharply with the driver shouting and making questioning gestures. Without hesitation, a glance, or even a break in his stride, the teenager removed a hand from his jogging bottoms and nonchalantly raised his middle finger towards the direction of the irate driver. Cam's reaction was one of despair, confirming in his mind that modern society has little room for thought or consideration.

Having finally found a car park, which unfortunately, charged extortionate rates, Cam exited his car and stretched his arms with his eyes closed. The relief of stretching and having stopped driving, momentarily made him feel like he was back in rural Lincolnshire. However, the sound of sirens echoing off the buildings within close proximity to him, soon brought him back to his senses and the reality that he wasn't in Lincolnshire. He immediately thought that he needed to wake up and switch on, he was fully aware that he was now in the city, and that anything could happen.

Chapter 2 The Meet

Making his way through the crowded streets to meet Neil, Cam did his very best to avoid contact with other pedestrians. He dodged, stepped aside and planned his every step. His resilience to being bumped and knocked had drastically waned as life steadily took its toll on him. So much so, that when he saw a group of youths walking towards him, he steadfastly decided that he wasn't going to allow himself to be diverted from his chosen course.

As the youths neared, he heard them laughing and talking in an accent that he would describe as 'illiterate speech'. Cam would describe it as speech where words are not started or finished correctly, or where sentences (the term used very loosely) are finished with an inappropriate question of 'in it?' or 'you know what I mean?' or that ever flexible word 'like'.'

The youths were dressed in what he would describe as their street uniform: a hoodie, jogging bottoms and an expensive pair of trainers. They also had what he would describe as their fashion accessory, a bum bag. He remembered it being made fashionable in the 1980s for a short time, then only being worn by what seemed like tourists but now being worn by every self-conscious teenager. Cam with his inquisitive, experienced and slightly sceptic mind thought that the bags were used to carry not only cash, cards and phones but also drugs. He considered the bags to be used like a statement to say, 'I've got some if you want some'.'

Now within feet of him, the group of six - consisting of two girls and four boys - did not appear as though they were going to alter course. Cam tensed every muscle in his body and continued on his course. A heavy thud was felt in his right shoulder and a lesser one in his left, he kept his eyes focused straight ahead to avoid any eye contact which may have been interpreted as a sign of aggression. The final youth passed, they all failed to break stride, direction or conversation with each other, just as though Cam did not exist. As he walked on Cam reflected on the situation. Although he had the slightest amount of satisfaction from not having to alter his stride or course, he felt a little ashamed of his behaviour and considered himself to have lost more than he had gained. He felt that it was an opportunity, unfortunately now passed, to have shown some courtesy by stepping to one side and potentially prompting an action of gratitude from the youths. He was totally aware that the chances of that happening were virtually non-existent, but by not giving the youths a chance to show it, now he'll never know. The more he reflected on it, the more he became ashamed of his behaviour, by failing to show the youths his natural good manners. This only increased his desire to leave the city as soon as he could. He was aware that the youths' behaviour was completely normal and acceptable in a city, he did not want to be accepting of the lack of courtesy and good manners.

Deep in thought, and very much keeping himself to himself, he continued to dodge the crowds. It was now nearing lunchtime and city workers were out in force trying to source their lunch, and with their time limited the last thing they were concerned about were good manners. Cam approached another street corner, just like the dozens he had already passed, but unknown to Cam this one would not pass unnoticed like the others. As he almost reached the corner he felt the full force of a person against his chest. The impact was so great it not only knocked all the air from his body but also knocked him clean off his feet. He could feel himself falling backwards, as though in slow motion, with this person appearing to be somehow fixed to his chest. After falling a few feet he felt his back hit a solid object, unknown to Cam it was a wooden gate to the rear yard of a pub. He felt the gate handle dig into his back, as the full force of him and his 'passenger' hit it. Fortunately for Cam the gate was old and rotting. It had an old bolt lock at the top and a spring in its centre to ensure the gate is always closed unless deliberately propped open. The impact of Cam and his unknown and unexpected passenger forced the bolt lock from the rotting wood and it flew open. Cam, with his passenger, didn't seem to lose much speed due to the impact, and flew through the gateway within a second. With life still in slow motion mode Cam saw the spring on the gate do what it was designed to do and close the gate immediately, he could see things, feel things and even smell things but he had no control over what was happening to him.

After what seemed like an eternity of falling backwards and having no control Cam, and his uninvited passenger, unceremoniously landed on the floor coming to an abrupt halt. He lay on his back, in pain, confused, disoriented and winded, life was still in slow motion mode. However, there was something that made everything else seem insignificant, it was the wonderful, sweet smell of perfume coming from his passenger. Within seconds he began to regain his senses, thoughts and composure and was overcome with concern for his sweet smelling passenger. He looked down at his chest and could see a light coloured woollen hat with locks of wavy black hair protruding from beneath it. Looking further down he saw a black coat that he would describe as a female donkey jacket, and even further down a pair of blue jeans. It was now very clear to him that he had been slammed to the floor by what appeared to be a very petite female. Cam was regaining the breath that had been knocked from him so was breathing heavily, but to his surprise his passenger's breathing was far louder and quicker than his.

"Are you ok?" Cam asked with a very concerned voice.

No response was forthcoming.

"Are you ok?" he asked again but louder this time.

"I'm so sorry, I'm so sorry, I didn't mean to knock you over. I was running and I tripped. I'm so sorry," came the reply in a delicate, frightened voice which had, what Cam thought to be, a hint of an Asian accent.

Cam was old school and very well-mannered, and because it was an unknown female apologising to him he automatically responded.

"It was my fault and I'm the one that should be apologising," he said.

Cam felt awkward and very uncomfortable and was unsure what to do, not because he laid on his back on the wet floor of a rear yard to an unknown pub, but because it had been a very long time since he had been in such close contact with a woman.

The unknown female, unaware of Cam's uncomfortable predicament that he didn't know how to solve, very delicately but hurriedly lifted herself off him and continued to apologise. Cam saw that the female was not much over five feet tall, slim build, approximately thirty years old with an Asian/Indian appearance. He thought that she was very pretty with an innocent look about her, as though life's troubles and pain had not yet had influence on her, a very rare thing in a city. As he slowly pulled himself from the floor he felt the pain in the centre of his back, which had been caused by the impact of the gate handle. He didn't know whether to feel embarrassed by being flattened by such a small lady or shocked that such a small lady could create so much force. Cam was a touch under six feet tall and of a solid build, weighing just under fifteen stone.

Eventually, both Cam and the female were on their feet and straightening their attire, eye contact was made several times, with both parties feeling a little uncomfortable about the situation and wondering how to resolve it. Cam eventually asked if the female had hurt herself, to which she informed him that she hadn't. The same question was reciprocated towards Cam to which he stated that he hadn't, although he had. He was suffering an amount of pain in his back still but would not disclose this, even he was unsure whether this was due to male pride, or his usual manner of not burdening others with his problems.

"Are you late for an appointment or something? Is that why you were running?" he asked.

He could see his questions had made the female uncomfortable so he tried to relax her by explaining his situation.

"I'm in London to meet a friend and if I don't hurry up I'll be late. I don't want to be late because I don't get to see him very often, also if I leave it too long I'll get caught in the rush hour traffic on the way out of London, and we all know what a nightmare that is. So if you're sure you are ok I'll get going," he said. Cam, half expecting a reply to endorse his intentions was a little taken aback and quite disappointed when a reply was forthcoming.

"I was being chased by two men, that's why I was running. I don't know who they are and I don't know why they were chasing me. I was so scared, I thought they were going to kill me. They looked so evil," she said.

At this she began to cry, Cam was searching his mind for a reasonable explanation to the situation, various options sprang to mind. Could she be a thief, he wondered? Inconspicuously, he checked for his wallet and car keys, they were still in his pocket. Did she push him in the yard deliberately so that her male accomplices could rob him at knife point? He quickly scanned the yard and saw that they were alone.

He came to the conclusion she was probably mistaken. Either the men were chasing somebody else and she wrongly thought they were chasing her, or they genuinely mistook her identity. Very plausible, he thought, especially if they were store detectives or security of sorts. On the balance of probabilities it appeared to be a mistake caused by confusion by one or more of the parties with no malice intended, he decided. With this in mind and hoping for a quick solution to this problem, which in his head had completely nothing to do with him, he decided he would attempt to calm the female and show her that there was no reason to be concerned. He then hoped to be swiftly on his way.

"What's your name?" he asked.

"Jasmina," she replied.

"My name is Cam. To ease your mind I'll come outside with you and hopefully you'll see that it was probably a case of mistaken identity. I need to be quick though because I don't want to keep my friend waiting. Is that ok?" he asked.

"Yes," she replied and added, "I'm so sorry."

As she spoke Cam recognised the fear in her eyes, he had seen it so many times before during his career. He also believed that the eyes were the gateway to a person's soul, the tongue may lie but the eyes cannot. This helped him come to terms with the fact he was doing something he did not particularly want to do, but the reason for doing it was sufficiently important.

They walked towards the gate. He saw that the bolt was on the floor. Cam thought he would phone the pub later, and if they needed to be reimbursed for the lock, Neil could pop in and pay them.

Cam opened the gate, stepped out and had a good look around. He couldn't see anybody running around as though they were looking for somebody, just crowds of people going about their business. It was a relatively busy, wide road, with traffic flowing in both directions. It was also very noisy due to traffic, people, and roadworks in the distance. He beckoned Jasmina out onto the street to have a look and put her mind at rest, she looked around for a few seconds and said nothing. In his mind, that was almost his cue to be on his way, he then heard a panic-stricken quivering voice speak.

"That's them," she said.

At this, she pointed to a dark coloured family-sized saloon car with two men sat in the front seats. The men were middle-aged and white, with short hair and wearing dark suits. Typical security, he thought.

Believing his assumption of mistaken identity to still be a probability, he informed Jasmina that he would go and speak to the men, to clarify the situation.

She waited by the gate, and Cam began to approach the car. By this time both men had seen Cam with Jasmina. As Cam neared the car it started up, this caused no concern to him as it was positioned in a parking bay facing onto the road and Cam was walking on the footpath. He thought the occupants may have wanted some heat from the engine as it was still a cold, wet day, so he continued to approach it. As Cam stepped from the footpath onto the road, the car suddenly accelerated towards him, slightly swerving in his direction and taking him by surprise, it drove straight at him. Although in his mid-fifties, his reactions were still very good, and he leapt away from the direction of the car.

As Cam was in mid-air he again had another feeling of things happening in slow motion, he felt a sharp pain in his lower leg and his body spun around approximately 90 degrees. The front nearside wing of the car had caught his left leg. Whilst travelling through the air he again had the feeling of total disorientation and pain, but overriding this was the disappointment that he would be late for Neil and his ever increasing dislike for cities.

Cam landed heavily on the road, his body landed with a dull thud, it stopped dead, this resulted in his head having a slingshot effect and crashing against the tarmac. The impact immediately knocked him unconscious, he lay there, still, and for all intents and purposes, dead to the world. For a few seconds, and a few seconds only, the crowds stopped to observe what was happening, but on realisation that it didn't disrupt their daily routine, they proceeded about their business.

Jasmina ran to Cam screaming for all she was worth and obviously thinking it was her fault that he was dead. Upon reaching him she realised he was breathing and not dead after all, she began to scream for use of a phone. Whilst trying to attract attention she could see that Cam had a large bump and graze to the left side of his forehead, this was obviously the place that took the impact, she also noticed his left lower leg was bleeding and blood was seeping through his jeans. Much to her disgust nobody volunteered use of their phone or called an ambulance for her.

After a few seconds of asking she searched Cam's pockets, found his phone and subsequently called for an ambulance. She comforted Cam, who obviously was completely unaware, and was subsequently joined by a couple of good spirited citizens who offered help and advice.

Feeling responsible for Cam, she just wanted do whatever she could to help.

CHAPTER 3 THE LITTLE WHITE LIE

Beep, beep, beep… "I think he's waking up now" were the first things Cam heard when he regained consciousness. As he slowly opened his eyes the first thing he focused on was a female nurse, she was a white lady aged about sixty with a friendly face. She had a calm, gentle demeanour but an authoritative voice.

Prior to considering why he was there, he felt pleased that he was in such good hands. As his eyes slowly scanned the cubicle he couldn't see any other patients but could hear them, some were laughing and joking, some were talking quietly as though not wanting to be heard, and some were complaining of pain. He realised he was in an accident and emergency department, he recognised the familiar sounds and indeed the smells. He could clearly smell disinfectant and blood mixed with alcohol. It had been many years since Cam had worked in uniform as a police officer but during that time he had been in an A&E department many times.

"Welcome back, Cameron. My name is Nurse Adams, you are in hospital in London. You've had an accident. We are looking after you and doing some tests at the moment to make sure you are ok. How do you feel?" said the nurse.

"My head feels a bit sore and my leg hurts. How did I get here?" he asked.

"You were brought in by an ambulance about an hour ago but you're doing really well. The doctor will be along shortly to speak to you. In the meantime if there's anything you need just ask and we'll do our very best to sort it for you. For now please try to relax," the nurse replied.

At this the nurse pulled back the cubicle curtain and swiftly disappeared. Whilst the curtain was pulled back, Cam saw an elderly gentleman aged approximately ninety years. He was sat in a wheelchair in the corridor looking totally confused, he had a graze and bump to his forehead. Cam

13

was unsure whether the confusion was caused by the injury or age. To Cam it mattered not, all he knew was that he felt sorry for the old gentleman. It appeared that he was on his own with no family or friends around him, just medical staff and the public rushing past him with their own concerns. They all passed him with no acknowledgement, as though he was a piece of furniture or completely invisible. Cam saw in the old gentlemen a possible vision of himself in the future. There was an acceptance of this within him which evoked mixed emotions, one of a strange form of contentment and the other, a simpler emotion to understand, fear.

Cam could see the old gentleman tiring, because with everybody that passed, he lifted his head as though to hear an explanation of why he was there, it was heart-breaking for Cam to witness this. The result of Cam witnessing the old gentlemen stirred contrasting emotions of his experiences in an accident and emergency department. He recalled many experiences, of which some were of a pleasant nature, like escorting pregnant women to hospital who were about to give birth. However, most were not of such happy times. Some people he'd had to deal with had been victims of assaults, sexual assaults and even murders.

He had not only seen and felt the suffering of victims, but also the cold unremorseful arrogance of offenders. Some had committed the most heinous of crimes but on their arrival at hospital expected to be treated with the same empathy, courtesy and dignity as their victims, and of course they were. Including his own behaviour, Cam had seen nothing but complete professionalism from hospital staff and his fellow colleagues during all the incidents he recollected. Fortunately for the hospital staff, most were never aware of the crimes their patients had committed. The same could not be said for Cam and his colleagues; matters of this nature are never forgotten by police officers, but are just another questioning of human nature that stays with them for life.

The curtain to Cam's cubicle was pulled back and a gentle but deep voice spoke.

"Mr Cameron Grant?" asked the doctor.

"That's me," Cam replied.

"I'm Doctor Freeman, can you please tell me how you are feeling?" he asked.

"I'm fine, doctor, when can I go home? Or at least can I phone my mate, Neil? I was supposed to meet him this afternoon," Cam replied.

It was obvious from Doctor Freeman's reaction that he was going to say "no". He delayed his reply to Cam for a couple of seconds and smirked a little. Cam's immediate impression of the doctor was one of approval. The doctor was an Afro-Caribbean, approximately fifty years of age, quite short in stature and very slim. He reminded Cam of the Rat Pack singer, Sammy Davis Junior.

"First things first," the doctor replied.

"Do you remember the accident you were involved in?"

Cam felt a little foolish, he had been so focused and concerned about the confused old gentleman, and worried about phoning Neil, he had not once thought about the accident.

He then thought about the accident for a few seconds and remembered it clearly.

"Yes I do, doctor, I was trying to help a lady, one that I had just literally bumped into, resolve her suspicion that she was being followed. I walked towards a car and it pulled away knocking me to the ground," Cam replied.

"Yes that's what the paramedics told us on your arrival. Did the car knock you over intentionally? Because if it did you must report it to the police as soon as you can, even if it was just an accident you must tell the police," the doctor stated.

Cam was fully aware of the law and his requirements in reporting accidents but did not want the doctor to feel bad about his advice.

"Yes, doctor, I will do so at the earliest opportunity, thank you. So does this mean I can go home now?" Cam asked.

"We just want to observe you for a little longer as you had quite a bump to your head. We also need to put a couple of stitches in your leg before you go," the doctor replied.

Cam reluctantly agreed to the doctor's suggestions, but knew deep down it was the only course of action the doctor could take, and the correct one. He couldn't possibly just let him walk out.

"Doctor, there's an old gentleman sat out there in a wheelchair, would it be possible for me to swap places with him so that he can have some peace and quiet in here?" Cam asked.

"Don't worry, Mr Grant, we have now placed him in a cubicle of his own but thank you for the offer," the doctor replied.

"Oh, would you like your wife to come through and sit with you while you wait?" he added.

Cam was completely astounded, he thought of no good reason why and how his ex-wife could be there. After all the bitterness and manipulation that had gone before, he could not understand her logic. He was of a mind to tell the doctor he didn't want to see her and to tell her to go home. However, the soft natural side of his personality came to the fore, and he convinced himself that it could be beneficial in resurrecting a relationship with his children if he spoke with her.

"Ok, doctor, you can send her through if you like," he replied.

Cam waited patiently in his hospital bed with his thoughts pondering over many things. He wondered who had been the person on his bed prior to him, were they young or old? Were they seriously ill, or like him, going to be out of there as soon as they could? Did they die? Whatever the question, he found the bed very comfortable indeed. It was firm, just how he liked it. He also recollected his times as a police officer again as the unmistakable and unforgettable smell of alcoholic drink mixed with congealed blood filtered through to his cubicle.

He saw a shadow reach towards the cubicle curtain and prepared himself for seeing his ex-wife for the first time in nearly three years. The curtain was being pulled back slowly, which seemed like an eternity for Cam. He just wanted to get the awkward meeting over and done with, hopefully resulting in some positivity regarding his children. He kept reminding himself to stay calm and not to get frustrated. The curtain finally went back and Cam just froze and stared at this woman who had entered his cubicle. He was completely confused and lost for words. It was not the figure of his ex-wife that stood there, but Jasmina, the beautiful Asian-looking woman that thought she was being chased.

His speech had left him momentarily, but his sense of smell definitely had not. He could smell her sweet perfume, he thought it was delightful outside in the fresh air, but in his cubicle it was all the more sweeter. It disguised the smell of disinfectant and blood, making it far less intrusive. His emotions couldn't decide what to feel: anger that it was Jasmina's influence that caused him to be lying there on a hospital bed, or to be pleased that she had waited there to see how he was.

"Thanks for waiting, I'm fine. I think you need to go now because my ex-wife wants to see me," Cam tried to explain.

"I'm sorry, they think I'm your wife because I travelled in with you on the ambulance and I gave them your details at the desk," Jasmina explained.

"How do you know who I am?" Cam asked, suspecting something underhanded or illegal.

"I used your phone to call for the ambulance and when I took your phone out of your pocket, your wallet fell out. To keep it safe I put it in my pocket because it has a zip fastener, yours clearly does not, you should take more care. When we got to the hospital I gave them your details from it without explaining how I got them," Jasmina explained.

She handed both his wallet and phone to Cam. He wanted to check it to see if all of the contents were there but he was far too polite. When the nurse entered the room to stitch Cam's leg, Jasmina, very politely and quickly left the cubicle telling Cam she would be in the waiting room.

Cam was shocked, confused and in a state of disbelief, not due to the accident or his injuries but because of the unexpected and seemingly honest actions of Jasmina. His mind explored all sorts of reasons for her impeccable behaviour and he started to feel as though she was totally honest and innocent. However, he deliberately held onto a degree of cynicism which again was part of his defence mechanism. He watched the nurse stitch his wound, a relatively deep cut of about two inches just on the outer side of his left shin which left the skin flapping a little. His thoughts were so deep about the day's events, it actually felt like he was watching the stitching procedure on TV instead of actually being performed on himself. Three stitches and a bandage later the nurse spoke.

"That's all done now, Cameron, I trust it doesn't feel too bad. I'll let the doctor know and he can then make an assessment on whether he feels you can go home," she said.

As she finished speaking she was already out of the cubicle which gave Cam no time to respond. It was the first time he had actually had to consider the staff may want to keep him there and not discharge him, this filled him with anxiety. It would mean that not only would he be away from his home, his place of tranquility, but also Colin, it saddened him to think of Colin being alone for so long. He knew Colin had enough food and water and had access to the garden but he still worried for him.

A few minutes after being stitched, Doctor Freeman entered the cubicle. Cam liked the doctor's demeanour which was very quiet, calm and deliberate.

"Ok, Mr Grant, I hope you're feeling a little better now that you've rested and been cleaned up. I am unsure as to whether to let you go home or keep you here for further observations," the doctor said.

Cam's heart sank.

"You see Mr Grant, although you may feel well now there is a possibility that you may take a turn for the worse later on. This sometimes happens with head injuries and I have to consider this," he added.

"I promise you I'm fine, doctor. There really is no need to keep me here, you could use your skills on somebody who needs treatment far more than I do," Cam said in an attempt to convince the doctor to discharge him.

Cam knew his opinion would stand little chance of influencing the doctor's decision and that it would be based on fact.

"If you were to go home, Mr Grant, is there anybody at home that could keep an eye on you and look after you?" the doctor asked.

Due to Cam's preferred lifestyle of being alone, there obviously wasn't. He frantically thought of friends or family who could fill this role of being a temporary carer, but there wasn't anybody. He was reluctant to ask anybody anyway because he did not wish to burden others with his problems.

He lifted his head and looked at the doctor and his thoughts appeared to bypass any filters between his brain and mouth.

"Yes, doctor, my wife is in the waiting area. I'm sure she won't mind keeping an eye on me," Cam said.

As soon as he said it he felt the weight of guilt had been placed upon him, but the thought of getting home and seeing Colin far outweighed its burden.

The doctor once again read Cam's notes and thought deeply, with no change in his expression he diverted his attention to Cam.

"Ok, Mr Grant, you can go home, but you must assure me that you take the medication that I'll prescribe for you. You must also promise that you visit your GP tomorrow for a check-up, and that in the meantime if you in any way start to feel ill, seek medical attention. Do you understand?" the doctor asked.

"Yes, doctor," Cam eagerly replied as though he was a boy on Christmas Eve, promising to go to sleep but having no real intention of doing so.

The doctor left the cubicle and Cam waited for his prescription, his conscience decided to do battle with itself. Firstly for telling an untruth to the doctor and secondly for involving Jasmina in it. How could he explain to her that she had been so significant in his deceit?

"There you are, Cameron," said the nurse as she entered the cubicle and handed a prescription to him.

"Make sure you take it steady on that leg for a few days and please make sure you follow the advice the doctor has given you. Also, I advise you not to drive," she added.

"Yes, nurse," he immediately replied.

"Can I go now?" he asked eagerly.

"Yes you're free to go," she replied.

"Thank you for all your help and I hope never to see you again," he said to the nurse with a smile on his face as he exited the cubicle.

Cam made his way to the waiting area to see Jasmina sat there. She could not see him so he stopped and looked at her for a while. She had removed the hat that she had been wearing earlier which revealed a mass of long, jet black wavy hair which dropped down to approximately six inches below her shoulders. His initial thought was that it must take a lot of washing and drying, but then he realised what a glorious and beautiful head of hair it was. Jasmina was still wearing the black donkey-type jacket and blue jeans she had been wearing earlier. What he hadn't noticed before, however, were the shoes she was wearing, they were black coloured flat shoes without socks underneath, his immediate thought was how inappropriate for the poor weather that day, she must be mad. His thoughts soon turned back to the task in hand, how do I tell this lady, who I don't know, who I've only spoken a handful of words to and who has patiently waited here to see if I'm ok, that I've involved her in my deceit by stating she was my wife so that I could selfishly go home? Oh well, he thought resiliently to himself, once I've apologised and thanked her for waiting, I won't ever see her again.

He approached Jasmina like a naughty schoolboy approaches a teacher knowing that he's going to get told off - slowly, full of shame and regret and in a very submissive manner.

"Hello, Jasmina," he said as he reached her.

She looked up at him with surprise. Cam could not help thinking how innocent and pleased she looked to see him. This did not help his feeling of guilt, and together with the fact that he was enjoying the smell of her sweet perfume again, only increased it.

"Hello, Mr Grant," she replied in a very formal manner, as though she was a burden to him and that he needed to be very forgiving towards her.

"Please call me Cam. I am in need of a very large cup of tea, there's something I need to tell you so would you like to join me?" he asked.

"Yes please, I am in need of a cup of tea too," she replied.

Cam and Jasmina left the hospital together, although not man and wife, but doing what many married couples do together, searching for a good cup of tea.

CHAPTER 4 THE INTRODUCTIONS

"Thank you very much," Cam said to the waitress, as she placed a large white teapot on the table.

Cam and Jasmina had found their way to a small cafe not too far from the hospital. It was rather small but very clean, it catered for people who wanted to sit, have a cup of tea or coffee and a chat. It was to Cam's taste, being not one of a chain of hundreds of trendy coffee shops. It was old-fashioned, quiet, with wood tables and chairs, personal service, and no crowds of people ordering a 'soya latte in a takeaway cup with a shot of caramel and syrup'. Cam was not bothered about what type of drink people wished to drink, or the type of people that ordered them. What he disliked was the amount of time people had to stand in, what appeared to be a never decreasing queue, wasting time. He wasn't an impatient man but did not like to needlessly waste time. The cafe was half-full with customers potentially waiting for the London rush hour to pass before braving the journey home. Cam and Jasmina were sat towards the back of the cafe where it was quieter, and furthest from the door. Soft classical music played in the background, Cam found this to be very soothing after the day he had endured.

Jasmina decide to pour the tea, she did it in a very controlled confident manner as though she was doing it in her home and not in a strange cafe, with a man who was a stranger, and under such strange and ridiculous circumstances.

"Jasmina, I really want you to listen to what I have to say and please let me finish before you react," Cam said to her expecting a negative and potentially angry reaction. "When I was in the hospital I did something which I am a little ashamed of, my reasons for doing it are that I am desperate to get home tonight. I live a few hours away and my dog has been on his own all day and as for me, I don't cope with cities at all well. The doctor wouldn't let me go home unless I had someone at home to look after me, and because they thought you were my wife I let them continue to think that for my own advantage. I feel awful, I feel guilty and I'm not proud of myself. I suppose you could say I'm just a sad fifty-five-year-old man who lives alone with his dog. I do hope you can forgive me, I have no right to ask, but I hope you can," Cam confessed.

Jasmina listened to Cam carefully and did not respond immediately, adding to Cam's stress. She sipped her tea, Cam watched her lips gently caress the cup and her hand delicately place it back on the saucer. Inside he was desperate for her to reply to his confession, firstly to ease his conscience, and secondly so he could get on his way home.

Perhaps as much as a minute passed but it seemed like an eternity to Cam. Eventually, Jasmina raised her gaze from her cup and looked Cam directly in the eye. Cam could not help but to maintain eye contact because although Jasmina had the biggest and most attractive green eyes he had ever seen, he saw in them something that he couldn't quite work out. He couldn't decide if it was fear, loneliness, a longing to be helped or something completely different.

"What you did was wrong, Cam, there is no getting away from that. However, due to the circumstances that you've explained I can understand your desperation to get home, no dog should be left on their own overnight. I forgive you, Cam, as there was no harm done to me and I am very thankful for your help earlier. My forgiveness is conditional, though, the conditions are that you please forgive me for involving you earlier and getting you injured. The second is that you listen to, and accept my explanation for bumping into you like I did," Jasmina stated.

Cam thought to himself that Jasmina's reaction was certainly better than he had expected. In his mind, Lincolnshire was getting ever closer, he could certainly listen to her reasons for bumping into him and forgive her.

"My name is Jasmina Singh, I am thirty-four years old. I live in Goa in India and I am a waitress in a hotel there. I now live on my own, I am not married and I have no children. This is the first time I have ever left Goa to travel anywhere," she explained to Cam in a very nervous and apologetic manner.

He maintained eye contact, still trying to work out what emotion he could see in her eyes, the eyes he felt like he was, ever more, being drawn into.

"Recently my mother, who I lived with, suddenly died from what I now know was a heart condition, she was only fifty-two years old. I had lived and worked with her all my life in the same hotel," she said. Jasmina's eyes started to fill with tears and her voice became a little broken and quieter. Cam, still staring into her eyes, now realised that amongst the fear and loneliness he saw earlier, he also saw grief. Cam had experienced grief first hand and seen it many, many times during his career, he could recognise it and understood the impact of it. He continued to listen attentively to Jasmina.

"I was at my mother's bedside when she died, it felt like my heart had been ripped out, I have never felt pain like it and I hope I never do again. She was all I had in life, all I ever wanted, and still do. I miss her so much."

Her eyes were now overflowing with tears, she began to sob and quiver, and looked so vulnerable. Cam immediately passed her a tissue and told her how sorry he was for her loss. He now had a decision to make, did he physically comfort this grieving, vulnerable lady and risk being misinterpreted for something more sinister? Or keep his distance, play safe and risk appearing to be an uncaring human being? Before he could make his decision his instinct took over, he reached out to hold Jasmina's hand that was already resting on the table. As he began to hold it he felt a slight resistance in her hand and immediately began to feel uncomfortable and a little presumptuous, however, the resistance lasted for only a second and then turned into something completely different, a definite grip of his hand.

He was full of mixed emotions himself by now. Her hand was cold, very delicate and small, and slightly shaking, he knew it was the correct thing to do in trying to comfort Jasmina. He could feel her sadness and desperation flowing into his body as though their hands were conductors of emotion. Cam's other emotion was one of comfort. It had been a long time since he had held the hand of a woman, inside him he could feel the joy of holding such a small delicate hand but also the guilt of enjoying the sensation in such circumstances.

"Minutes before she died she wanted to tell me something. But by this time she was very weak and breathless. I knelt down by the bed and put my ear next to her mouth, she whispered four words to me, "'my drawer, your father'". At the time I thought she was confused and did not know what she was saying. Almost immediately she developed a smile on her face, the type you have when you experience complete happiness. She looked so beautiful when she smiled. I had never seen her smile that way before, I had seen her smile thousands of times but never that way. She then died, still with that smile on her face. I am sure she died thinking of my father, do you think she did?" she asked Cam.

Cam was now full of thoughtful emotion himself and had tears filling his eyes. He needed to wait a second or two before replying because he knew his voice would have quivered.

"It certainly sounds that way, Jasmina and I hope you're right. I'm sure it was very important for you and your mother that you were there at that time. How is your father?" he asked.

"That's why I am in London, Cam, to find him and tell him. I knew nothing about my father until I searched in my mother's drawer. There I found a photo of her with this handsome man, she had that exact same smile on her face as she did when she died. My mother looked about 18 years old and the man looked a bit older."

As she spoke she placed the photo on the table, it was indeed an old photo but one that had obviously been cared for. Cam's impression of the two people in the photo was that they were extremely happy together, and at that moment in time, for them, nothing else mattered. To Cam, Jasmina's mother appeared to be a beautiful Indian lady, some would say just a girl, and the man appeared to be in his mid-twenties. He would describe the man as being white European and very formally dressed, whilst Jasmina's mother was clothed in more traditional Indian attire. In the background of the photo was a prominent sign which read 'Hotel Jasmin' and underneath it 'Goa'.

"If you've never met your father how do you intend to find him, and why are you in London?" Cam asked.

"After finding the photo I showed it to my aunt, my mother's older sister and she immediately started to cry. I knew instantly that the man in the photo was my father. She told me that his name was Thomas Allan, that he was from London, and in Goa on a business trip when he met my mother. She informed me that she was the one who took the photo. My mother was a cleaner at the hotel where we live, sorry, where I live and he was there with his father, they were in the process of buying the hotel. My aunt told me that they had fallen in love almost immediately and were inseparable, she said their romance was like one of those you see in a film and that they were full of love and optimism. She said that even though there was such a big difference in their cultures, wealth and backgrounds, it just didn't matter to them. My father was there for a month before he had to return to London with his father. It must have been so very difficult for my mother, because on the night before he left they had arranged a picnic on the beach, but she was made to work, she missed saying goodbye and planning their future. That was the last she saw or heard of him. She believed that because she failed to show on his last night, my dad thought that she didn't care and didn't want any further contact," Jasmina explained.

Cam went silent for a few seconds, digesting the information he had just been given. It was almost enough information to overload his emotional state. He was in turmoil about being so sad for Jasmina but thankful that he had known his parents, and his children knew him.

"So I take it your father doesn't know you exist?" he asked.

"I don't think so but I don't know for certain. My mother never made it common knowledge who my father was, even I didn't know. I know now from my aunt that my father was the only boyfriend my mother ever had, she was so heartbroken when he left and still in love with him when she died," she replied.

"How do you know he's in London?" Cam asked.

"I am not sure but the company his father owned was A. H. L. G., they are based here and still own Hotel Jasmin," she replied.

"Couldn't you have phoned him and saved yourself the bother of travelling all this way?" Cam asked.

"I need to tell him face to face that my mother has died, she is worth that, and I will tell by his reaction if he loved her or not. If he loved her I will tell him of my existence but if he didn't love her, I won't," she replied.

Cam knew of the company Jasmina spoke of, Allan Hotel and Leisure Group, it was a big concern which owned hotels and leisure complexes worldwide. He feared for Jasmina's quest because even if she did get to speak to her alleged father face to face, he may have forgotten about his holiday romance or deny it.

"How do you plan to speak to him?" Cam asked nervously.

"I tried today," she replied as she wiped tears from her eyes again.

Cam had already wiped his tears away by pretending to sneeze, he didn't want Jasmina to feel any worse than she already did.

"I went to The Allan Hotel where the business is registered. I only got as far as the receptionist. I asked if I could speak to Thomas Allan and was subsequently asked the nature of my business, I could only reply that it was of a personal nature. The receptionist took my name, the name of the hotel where I'm staying and my phone number. She informed me that the message would be passed onto him. She didn't seem to take much notice and was very casual about it, although I thought the other lady might take some action because as soon as I said my business was personal she became very interested in me. I noticed that when I was leaving the reception area she immediately left her office and went straight to the receptionist. I thought she'd sort it because she appeared to be management, her office had glass walls and sat above the reception area so that she could see everything. I thought she must have a speaker in her office that listens to everything that's being said in reception. She was also smartly dressed and looked very important," she replied.

"Well that does sound promising, I trust you've not heard anything as yet?" Cam asked.

"No I haven't. As soon as I had finished at The Allan Hotel, I went straight back to my room at the Tate Hotel for a rest, but when I got there I found it had been burgled. Nothing had been stolen because I had all of my important stuff with me - purse, passport and phone - to be honest other than that I have only brought a few clothes. The thing that really upset me was that I had a copy of this photo," she said as she pointed to the one of her mother and potential father, "and it had been torn up and left on the side. I don't understand why anybody would do that. Do you?" Jasmina asked Cam.

"Not really," he replied.

"I was so upset and didn't know what to do, so I decided to go for a walk and calm down. That's when those two men, the ones who were in that car, started to follow me. At first I didn't take any notice, but they kept making me aware of their presence, as though they were teasing me. They frightened me, I didn't know what to do so I just ran as fast and as far as I could, but they just kept following me. My phone fell out of my pocket whilst I was running but I was too scared to stop and pick it up. I really thought they were going to kill me. Why me? What have I done wrong to deserve this? I'm so scared. Anyway, that's when I bumped into you," Jasmina said.

"Wow, no wonder you were running if you were so scared. If there was anything I could do to help you I would, but I'm not sure I can," Cam stated.

"I'm not asking for your help, I was just explaining how I bumped into you, to show you I didn't do it intentionally," Jasmina clarified.

"What are you going to do tonight?" Cam asked.

"I will go back to the hotel, I'm sure they wouldn't have gone back there now they know there's nothing there to steal," Jasmina replied.

"You must report this to the police, they'll check the room for you." Cam advised.

"I'll do it in the morning, I think. I'm so tired now. I'll do it after I've been back to The Allan Hotel tomorrow," Jasmina stated.

"We've been talking for over an hour now and I know you have a long drive home so I think I'll let you get off now. Thank you for listening to me and hopefully understanding why I was so distressed," she added.

They both stood up to leave the cafe. Cam left enough money on the table to cover the bill and they both made their way towards the door. Cam was still digesting the information he had been told, and worrying about Colin, but very much looking forward to getting home. As they exited the cafe they both stood on the pavement directly outside facing each other. Jasmina put her hat back on and Cam fastened his duffle coat.

"Thank you again, Cam, for understanding, I hope you have a safe journey home and that your dog is ok," Jasmina said.

"Thank you and I hope everything works out for you," Cam said.

When they finished speaking, they just stood opposite each other, looking at each other, but trying not to. There was an awkwardness about the situation and their predicament. They both wanted to leave, but at the same time didn't. They eventually turned their backs on each other and started walking, going their separate ways. There was no doubt that both Cam and Jasmina were better people for having spent time in each other's company.

Cam continued to walk towards his car, pondering not only how much his car parking would cost him, but also if the rush hour traffic had calmed down. He phoned Neil and explained to him the unforeseen events of the day. This made Cam reflect on the day too, and also his behaviour.

The day's events and the head injury made him feel as though he couldn't think straight or make a decision. The fresh air, after coming out of the cafe, made Cam's nose run a little, making him sniff. He took a large sniff and much to his disbelief and joy, he could smell the sweet perfume of Jasmina. He was unsure if he was actually smelling it, or if it was down to his imagination, either way, it shocked him to his senses.

He questioned what he was doing and why he was going home. There's a young lady, all alone in a strange country, looking for her father, and still grieving for her mother, he reminded himself. He knew he wouldn't be able to live with himself if he walked away leaving her to face her problems alone. He immediately turned around and hurried, as quick as his injured leg would let him, towards where he had parted company with Jasmina. He could still move well for a man of his age, and after a minute or so he reached the cafe, looked up and down the road in both directions hoping to see Jasmina, but he couldn't. His heart sank somewhat, but he refused to lose faith and hurried off like a hobbling, possessed man in the direction that she had walked. After approximately a quarter of a mile or so he stopped, for two reasons. Firstly, he was convinced that Jasmina couldn't have reached that far on foot. Secondly, he was completely exhausted and out of breath.

He subsequently began to make his way back to his trusted VW, contemplating the day and his own actions regarding Jasmina. He was very disappointed with himself. He passed the cafe where, only a short time before, he had witnessed a lonely young woman pour out her soul to him. He felt increasingly disgusted with himself. Why didn't I help more, he thought to himself whilst looking at his feet treading on the dark wet pavement? A slight movement in his peripheral vision caught his attention, and on further examination he saw a sight that potentially would give him redemption. It was Jasmina, sat in the same seat, in the same cafe, he couldn't believe how fortunate he was. He nervously entered the cafe not knowing what reception he would get from Jasmina. He needn't have worried. Upon seeing him she immediately got up and made her way towards him. He looked into her big green eyes and saw them fill with tears. He, too, couldn't hold back his tears of relief. As they hugged, Cam felt the warmth of a log fire, the comfort and familiarity of an old armchair, the trust of a lifelong friend and the excitement of watching your child being born. For some reason he felt like he was where he belonged, he was sure Jasmina felt it too. After unlocking their grip on each other, Cam looked directly into Jasmina's eyes with all the protectiveness and sincerity imaginable.

"I can't let you stay here, you are coming home with me!" he said.

"Ok I will. Back home people love and try to help each other. What I've seen of this country so far it doesn't appear that way here. We can give our love and trust, with very little chance of it being abused and destroyed. Everybody here seems to be interested only in money, material possessions and hurting each other. I feel so different and very much alone, like I just don't fit in," she replied.

Jasmina, not realising it, had just informed Cam of how very similar they both were. They were words that he would never forget.

CHAPTER 5 THE PROMISE

"Mind where you step," Cam said to Jasmina.

They had arrived at Cam's home, it was dark, wet and cold. The journey had been a long one and they were both tired and hungry. Although his VW was a trusted, reliable 'friend', it was not the most luxurious of cars.

"I leave food out for hedgehogs and sometimes they are hard to see. I'll put the outside light on and then you'll be able to see where you're treading," he added.

Jasmina looked rather dishevelled as she stepped out of the car, her coat was done up tightly around her neck, as far as it could go, her hat was pulled down as low as it could go without covering her eyes and she had Colin's car blanket wrapped around her. Colin always had his blanket on the back seat of the car. As the light came on she looked around her and saw Cam's house and garden, she thought to herself this was pretty much what she expected on the outside. The garden was very functional and low maintenance with a gravelled area on which was situated a bench. The bench faced away from the bungalow and unknown to her it offered beautiful views when in use. The front door was oak, Cam had bought it from a salvage yard due to it looking very old and rustic, much unlike the rest of his bungalow which looked very functional.

"Please come in and make yourself at home. I'll get the log burner fired up in a minute," Cam said as Jasmina approached the door.

Once inside Jasmina's senses became very active. She scanned the hallway and living room, the first thing she noticed was the smell of dog, Colin to be precise, it was not a strong odour, but to anybody who doesn't own a dog, it's obviously far more noticeable. She thought to herself that it was a typical single man's home, in need of a dusting, no articles or pieces of furniture that were there for purely cosmetic purposes, they were all functional and appeared well used. The only things that appeared to have any other use, apart from functionality, were some framed photos of Cam, his parents and his children. Jasmina correctly assumed they were his children. Cam entered the living room to where Jasmina was stood, he was directly followed in by Colin. Colin, always on the hunt for a fuss, made his way to Jasmina and after sniffing her legs briefly, rolled onto his back in front of her expecting to be fussed.

"Take no notice of him, he'll go back to his bed if you ignore him. Please sit down, I'll soon have this fired up," Cam said as he walked towards the log burner with a basket full of logs.

"Who are the photos of, Cam?" she asked.

"Those are my children, and they are my parents, Richard and Maisie. Unfortunately, they are no longer with us," he replied.

"Lovely names, do you miss them?" she asked.

"I do, but I'm glad they were not here to witness all the trouble I've had with my children, it would have broken their hearts," he replied.

Cam saw a questioning look on the face of Jasmina. He assumed that she was inquisitive regarding their age, and the manner in which they died.

"They died in a car crash that wasn't their fault. It happened almost ten years ago, just before Christmas. They had driven over to see me and the children, bringing their presents. They always went over the top at Christmas. On their way home, whilst driving down a country lane, a car lost control on a bend and crashed into them, killing them both. They didn't stand a chance due to the speed of the other car. The driver of the other car wasn't local and didn't know the roads, he had travelled to an office Christmas party and drank too much. After his post-mortem they found he was three times over the drink driving limit," he added whilst setting the fire in the log burner.

Jasmina could see that Cam had become very thoughtful about his parents. Although wanting to know more about them and how he felt, she knew that they were both tired and didn't want to upset him further, so let the conversation finish. She looked for the seat which was closest to the log burner, it was an old-fashioned armchair with a high back and a throw over it - a mix of blanket and fleece material, the type which keeps you warm on cold nights such as this. She sat down, still with her coat done up and Colin's car blanket wrapped around her. As the log burner hissed and smoked its way into life the flames began to flicker, this immediately made Jasmina feel a little warmer, she knew it was psychological but it was effective. As the smoke cleared from the log burner it revealed larger flames and the crackle of the burning wood became louder. The heat began to exude from it and by this time it was not psychological, she could actually feel the heat and began to warm up, as she did her body became a little less tense, as did her mind. The flames became hypnotic and she could feel her mind wandering as she became ever more absorbed by them.

"I'll put the kettle on and we can have a hot brew, you can't beat a good brew. Sorry, I mean a cup of tea," Cam said.

"Ok, that would be lovely," she replied.

"If you're hungry I can do us some beans on toast, if you fancy it, I know I do," Cam said.

"That sounds lovely," Jasmina replied.

Cam entered the kitchen and was thankful that Jasmina agreed to toast, as he only had stale bread. The smell of toast, beans and a fresh pot of tea soon filtered through to where Jasmina was sat. They comforted her because the smells were one of the most normal things that had occurred that day, the comfort of familiarity. Her eyes still focused on the fire as she pondered the events of the day and how she had ended up in the house of a stranger, in a strange county in a strange country. It was quite the opposite to what she had planned for her first trip away from Goa.

"You may want to take your coat off, I'm about to bring the food in," Cam yelled.

At this, Jasmina started to take her coat off hoping that she wouldn't start shivering again. She discovered quite the opposite, in fact, and when she removed Colin's car blanket and her coat, the heat from the log burner seemed to penetrate her bones. The warmth gave her a feeling of security.

Cam entered the room with his offerings, beans on toast and mugs of tea on trays, and delicately placed the tray on Jasmina's lap in the hope that it met her expectations. He needn't have worried, Jasmina finished her meal before he had. Both Jasmina and Cam seemed unable to speak after eating their meals and drinking their mugs of tea. They just sat there as if they were wallowing in the satisfaction of having a full stomach, peace and quiet, but most of all, the warmth of the log burner.

After approximately fifteen minutes or so of staring into the log burner, Cam stirred and stood up, he stretched and closed his eyes and sighed out of contentment.

"I'm having another mug of tea, would you like one?" he asked Jasmina.

"I would, yes please. I'll come and help you," she replied.

Both made their way to the kitchen, carrying the empty plates and mugs with them. The kitchen was small and basic, Cam had furnished it the way he wanted, with all freestanding furniture. It was, as you would expect in his home, functional but with some weird character. Cam commenced to make the tea and Jasmina began to wash up, she laid hands on everything without the need to ask. It was a strange sensation for Cam, not only sharing his kitchen with a woman he'd only met that day, but with one that made him feel so many emotions at the same time. He felt relaxed but tense, sad but happy, confused but clear of mind, but most of all he felt comfortable but uncomfortable. His emotions were exacerbated whenever he smelt Jasmina's perfume, It reminded him of the pleasures of being in female company. In such a tight kitchen, it was inevitable that their bodies would come in close proximity to each other. This made Cam feel like a schoolboy in relation of not knowing know how to act, if he should apologise, ignore it as if nothing had happened or give prior warning when he wanted to move. He had no idea of the impact this had on Jasmina, she gave no indication.

Both survived their close encounters in the kitchen and returned to the lounge with their mugs of tea, by this time its temperature could only be described as toasty, the heat hit their faces as they entered. As they sat, and again became hypnotised by the flames of the log burner, Cam felt many questions come to his thoughts about the day's events. He knew that it wasn't the appropriate time for him to ask or her to answer any questions.

"I'm sure today has been as traumatic for you as it has been for me, we can talk in the morning about your situation, but for now I'm happy that you are safe and well for tonight. I could not leave you in that desperate state in London. Whilst you're here please treat my home as if it were yours. If there's anything you need, and if you can find it, please help yourself," Cam stated.

"Thank you, Cam, you have been, sorry, you are so kind. I don't think I can ever repay you. I felt so lonely in London, it's much better here. I will try to not get in your way," she said.

Again, Cam felt strange. Between them they had silences but they were comfortable silences, not awkward. He knew that some people can live a lifetime together and never have a comfortable silence. He was trying very hard to understand his own emotions, eventually putting them down to the knock he had to his head.

The time soon arrived for them to retire to bed and get some much needed sleep.

"If you sleep in my bed I'll get my head down on the settee. The heating should have warmed the bedroom a little by now so it shouldn't feel too cold, however, if you feel the need to wear something to sleep in, there are clean T-shirts and jogging bottoms in the drawers somewhere, you're welcome to use them. In the bathroom there is a brand new toothbrush, I keep it just one case one of the grandkids decide they would like to stay, please use it," he said.

"Thank you," she replied in a very grateful, almost submissive, manner.

Cam settled Colin down for the night, stocked up the log burner and closed the vents to obtain a slow burn, this would keep some warmth in the bungalow during the night. He fetched his sleeping bag from the cupboard in the hallway and placed it on the settee. Cam had slept many times on the settee, usually due to not being able to sleep, he was used to staring into the flames and waiting for them to provide solutions to his problems. This was potentially going to be one of those nights. Jasmina exited the bathroom wearing a grey coloured sweatshirt and jogging bottoms, it was fair to say that they almost buried her. Cam looked at her and thought she looked so vulnerable, as thought she had the weight of the world, undeservedly, placed upon her shoulders. This made him want to hug and comfort her, to provide her with some reassurance, but he resisted. He thought that it could, due to the time of night, be misinterpreted as though he was trying to take advantage.

"Jasmina, I know you have lots of questions that need answers in relation to your father - they may, or may not get answered. After a good night's sleep we can both put our heads together and try to find some answers, we may not find any but we can try," Cam said.

On hearing this, Jasmina's mood changed a little, she immediately appeared to be more positive.

"Do you mean you'll help me? Will you? I don't expect you to but if you could it would very much appreciated," she said.

Cam, on seeing her reaction to his suggestion, had mixed thoughts himself. He felt good that his words had provided some positivity and optimism to Jasmina, but he was also aware that his assistance may not achieve anything.

"I've said I'll try to help, so I will. I promise," he said.

Cam was the type of person who liked to keep his promises. As he finished speaking, Jasmina walked to him and hugged him, it had the same effect as it did in the cafe, giving him many, mixed emotions. This is certainly not what he wanted just prior to retiring to bed. When she hugged him this time, without all the outdoor clothing on, he could feel the contours of her body against his. She felt like a woman and not just a person. Due to the height difference, and with her arms placed tightly around his neck, she was on tiptoes, pulling her body weight towards his. Cam could feel the warmth from her body, her breath on his ear and the sweet smell of her perfume. The feeling of her petite but very feminine body against his stimulated feelings within Cam that he had not felt for years, including desire. He did not know where to hold her, should he put his hands on her waist so that he could hold her at a distance and hide the obvious fact that he was very sexually stimulated, or should he not hold her at all, therefore giving her no reason to think ill of him? It was too late, his brain did not react in time and the natural desire of his body did what it wanted to do. He put his arms around Jasmina and held her tight.

At some point he expected her to pull away and ask him what he thought he was doing. To his surprise, and pleasure, she didn't. It was obvious to Cam that she could clearly feel his erection pressing against her body, she did not move. Perhaps she's too tired to move, perhaps she's too scared to move, perhaps when we stop hugging she'll run out of the house shouting abuse at me, he thought. However, he remained in hold, still feeling her body against his. Again, he was unsure what it was, but something of significance, in addition to the uncontrollable physical reactions, was happening between them. He considered the options of what they were sharing; friendship, trust, reassurance or complete exhaustion.

After five minutes of hugging, their embrace loosened and both stood back. Cam was hoping that Jasmina would not mention the state of his sexual arousal and that, whatever he felt during their embrace, it wouldn't be lost. They focused on each other's faces. Cam felt like Jasmina had transformed from an uncertain, slightly scared female, into a confident, self-assured woman. In his eyes she looked radiant and soft, her demeanour appeared to have changed. She leant forward and kissed him on the cheek, he could feel her breath and smell her perfume again.

"Thank you," she said, in a soft genuine voice.

Cam was unsure what she was thanking him for but he was thankful for the feeling of her soft lips against his cheek.

"You're welcome," he replied.

Jasmina made her way to the bedroom, Cam, whilst watching her walk away, couldn't help but wonder how it would feel to hold her all night, skin to skin. As the door closed to her bedroom he made his way to the bathroom and then the settee where he immediately got into his sleeping bag.

Although feeling a little guilty for the way he had just felt in relation to Jasmina, he also felt rather proud and pleased that he had acted as gentlemanly as he did. He thought that if anything else had developed, not only would it have had a detrimental effect on him and how he thought of himself, but it potentially may have had a catastrophic effect on Jasmina due to her situation. He convinced himself that in a few days Jasmina would be on her way home having solved her issues. He did not want her emotions tossed about any more than they had been already. He knew the outcome of their embrace was the only sensible one. He also did not want any confusion, complication or senseless emotion in his life. He did, however, realise that the bed sheets on his bed had been on there a few days, he began to worry what Jasmina might think of him, he did not want her to think that he was slovenly and dirty.

Looking into the flames be began to reflect on the day and the effect it had had on him. He sought answers from the flames regarding Jasmina's situation until his eyes could take no more, the last thought he had that day was of the promise he had made to Jasmina.

CHAPTER 6 THE PLAN

The following morning, Cam woke at his usual time of approximately 6.30. He gently straightened his back and legs after having been, what felt like at times, restrained in his sleeping bag all night. Before opening his eyes he could hear the resident blackbird in full voice, this immediately filled his heart with joy, so much so that he decided to lay a while and listen to its chorus. Whilst stretching and placing his 'manhood' in its correct position he decided that he had kept his eyes closed long enough. He opened them, still with a little smile on his face, and saw what he sees most mornings, Colin staring at him. Slowly his eyes focused on Colin as he spoke to him.

"Morning, Colin," he muttered in an early morning, croaky voice.

As he opened his mouth he could smell his morning breath, which isn't pleasant on anybody, especially when mixed with a little smoke from the log burner and Colin's morning breath. His eyes were near normal focus now and they immediately readjusted to something that was further back from his view than Colin, it was Jasmina. She was stood in the doorway to the kitchen with a tea towel in her hand. Still dressed in the grey coloured sweatshirt and jogging bottoms, she wore a cute little smile on her face which appeared to be induced by observing Cam go through his morning routine of waking up.

"Good morning, Cam. I hope you slept well because I certainly did," she said.

Cam was not used to seeing a woman upon waking up and was a little shocked, he immediately began to recall the events of yesterday.

"Good morning, Jasmina. I slept ok. I'm glad you slept well," he replied.

His eyes were fully focused on Jasmina now, she looked completely refreshed, her eyes were wide and bright, her hair was even more wavy and shiny, he thought she glowed. He tried to dismiss the thought from his mind but he looked at her and fully appreciated how beautiful she was.

Again, he did not know how to respond to his natural feelings and observations of Jasmina, it was as though all of his common sense, and experience of dealing with situations, abandoned him every time she was in his presence.

"I've done us some eggs on toast and a pot of what you call 'brew'. I hope that's ok," she said.

It had been a long time since anyone had cooked Cam breakfast, he was thrilled, embarrassed and grateful all at the same time.

"That sounds wonderful. I am due to do some shopping in case you're wondering why there's no food in the cupboards," he replied, trying to provide an excuse for his embarrassment of having so very little choice of food.

"Don't worry. I was raised to believe that it is greedy to want more than you need and I am still a believer of that. In Hotel Jasmin, where I work, there is so much waste. It saddens me when there is so much hunger in the world," she said.

Cam was rather taken back by her attitude, he had said almost the same thing to many other people and always been told that he was miserable and needed to lighten up. He was thrilled that somebody he knew thought the same way as he did. By this time Jasmina had gone back into the kitchen and he could hear her plating up. He quickly scrambled from his sleeping bag, pulled on his jeans, and headed to the bathroom to save Jasmina noticing the physical thing that happens to most men in the morning. On exiting the bathroom he saw that Jasmina had placed his food next to the settee, she was sitting in the chair next to the log burner eating her breakfast.

"I am very thankful for this, it looks lovely," Cam said as he walked towards his breakfast.

"I truly believe that the more you own, the more you have to worry about," he added with reference to the earlier conversation.

Just before sitting down he placed some logs on the burner and Jasmina smiled at him as if to say, 'how did you know what I was thinking?'.

They both stayed silent for a while whilst eating their breakfast, so as not to disturb each other. As Cam ate his food he couldn't help but look at Jasmina's feet. He was a man who could pick fault with most people's feet as he found them most unattractive, especially if uncared for. He looked and could not pick fault, again they were petite, all in proportion and with her toenails perfectly painted. Is there no fault with this woman, he asked himself?

"I've been thinking about your situation and how to approach it. I have thought of a plan to see if we can get to your father and see if he's prepared to talk to you. Are you ready to hear it? I don't want to rush you," Cam said.

"Yes, Cam, that would be great. Any help would be most appreciated but whilst you're talking can I attend to the graze on your forehead and have a look at your leg?" she replied.

He readily agreed because had if it been left to him he would have forgotten about it and probably wouldn't have been bothered to do anything with them.

"Lie on the settee and I'll get some water," she said.

Cam positioned himself on the settee, he lost all sense of awkwardness due to him putting his 'detective' head on. When he was a detective he always did things thoroughly and to the very best of his ability, in his eyes this task was no different.

"I've been thinking, your dad must be at least fifty-nine or sixty years old now. It's not too unreasonable to think that he may be retired or semi-retired. I'm sure if he had died you would have heard, as his company owns the hotel you work in, so we can assume that he is still alive. There is a possibility that he lives abroad in a warmer climate though," Cam said.

"I wouldn't blame him for that," Jasmina stated as she entered the lounge with a bowl of water, cotton wool and a towel.

Cam looked at the cotton wool curiously and realised he didn't even know that he had any.

"I laid last night going through all different scenarios in my head and the most feasible one, without coincidence playing a major part, is the one where people have tried to scare you off. I don't know why, but I'm guessing that the smart lady who had the glass office had something to do with it, because only she, and the receptionist, knew your details and where you were staying. If, and I haven't checked it yet, the Tate Hotel is part of A. H. L. G., then this smartly dressed female would have had access to your room without causing damage or suspicion. As only your photo was damaged and nothing was stolen, we can assume that this has something to do with your quest of finding your father. I think the two men who followed you just tried to scare you off, not hurt you and definitely not kill you. If they wanted to hurt you they would have done it in the privacy of the hotel room, where there could be no witnesses, and if a mess had been caused it could have been cleaned up easily without leaving any forensic evidence. I don't know why they have done this but from my experience I think it's down to greed or somebody trying to hide something," he said.

"I don't know what to say. I have nothing that they can take from me and I don't know any secrets," Jasmina replied in a worried manner.

"I don't think for one minute that you have anything to hide or steal. It could be that you are the secret that your father is trying to hide," Cam said.

"I don't think my father knows about me and if he did, why would he try to hide me?" she asked.

"I don't know, Jasmina, perhaps he has a jealous wife and doesn't want her to find out about you and his love affair with your mother. It's just guesswork at the moment, however, we have two ways of trying to find out. We could try ourselves or we could just go to the police, I have to go and report the accident anyway," Cam stated.

"I can't go to the police, I'm afraid I didn't have a passport when my mother died and I decided to come here, so I borrowed my friend's, she is also a waitress at the hotel. If I go to the police they'll find out and they'll deport me," she stated.

"Ok then, that solves two dilemmas, we don't go to the police about your burglary and father, it also means we won't report the accident because you are the main witness and I don't want those men knowing who I am, or where I live. We are on our own then," he stated.

"I know you said you would help me, Cam, but hearing what you've just told me I'll understand if you don't want to," Jasmina replied.

"I promised I would help you and I will, so don't worry. I never thought I would have to do some detective work ever again, so it will be different and a nice change for me. I'll make us another brew," he said, as he got up to walk to the kitchen.

"The good thing is that they now probably think you have gone away, especially as you didn't go back to the hotel last night. Unfortunately, that means that you either find another hotel, one that's definitely not in their hotel group, or you stay here. I promise you that you'll not be in my way, in fact, it would be a pleasure to have you here and it would mean we could discuss our plans far more easily," he said as he entered the kitchen.

Cam was quite relieved he was out of sight because he hoped that Jasmina would agree to his suggestion of staying at his, he did not want her to see the disappointment on his face if she suggested otherwise.

"If it's no problem I would like to stay here, you make me feel so comfortable and welcome. So yes, I will stay with you," she stated.

He had no right to be but Cam was so very pleased. Although she'll be back in India in a few days' time, he thought, the few days she spends here will make my time so much more pleasurable.

"Anyway, Cam, when you come back with the tea you need to lie on the settee so I can look at your wounds. We have been so engrossed in conversation that I forgot to do them," she stated.

He took the tea into the lounge and followed his instructions by lying on the settee. Jasmina soaked the cotton wool in what now was tepid water, and began to cleanse the graze on his head, she wiped it gently with a high level of concentration. Due to her gaze being fixed on his forehead, the opportunity arose for Cam to stare straight into her large green eyes. His gaze was so intense it was almost as though he was searching them. As we know, he believes the eyes are the gateway to a person's soul. Cam didn't do much searching in her eyes, he got lost in them, and not for the first time.

Yet again he became the 'guilty schoolboy' trying not to let Jasmina see him looking. Her gaze diverted from the wound and straight to his eyes, he blushed a little as she had a knowing smile on her face.

"How does that feel?" she asked.

"Not too bad," he replied.

In his mind he was thinking it felt absolutely fantastic. When you touch me I feel amazing, he thought. But obviously he could not tell her that.

Jasmina pulled up the leg of his jeans as far as it could go but it wouldn't rise above the bandage. Cam felt an awkwardness regarding the question that may, or may not, be forthcoming.

"Can you take your jeans off?" Jasmina asked.

That was the question he thought might be asked. What do I do now? I've not showered. I've got yesterday's underwear on and I don't know if I smell or not, he thought to himself. Cam stood up and removed his jeans and quickly laid back down. Jasmina removed the bandage on his leg to reveal his stitches. They didn't look too bad to Cam, he had seen, and had, far worse injuries.

Jasmina put some antiseptic around the wound - some old stuff that she had found in the kitchen - and began to dress it again with a towel that she had cut into strips. Cam was amazed at the amount of intuition she had, she seemed to do everything in a calm, methodical manner. He could not see her being bullied or rushed into anything, she was petite, but in Cam's estimation, had the spirit of a giant.

"How does that feel now?" she asked in relation to his leg.

"Fine, it feels fine, thank you," he replied, feeling quite pleased with himself that he had controlled his emotions.

"Good. I'll just clean all this blood from your leg and then you're done," she said.

Jasmina began to clean his leg with the cotton wool and water, Cam watched and noticed, unsure if it was his imagination, or not, that she did it so slowly and in such long strokes, as if she was teasing him. Whether she was or she wasn't, Cam felt himself in that position again, the one that she often placed him in, having little or no control of his emotions. Cam could feel himself getting sexually aroused, he tried to make conversation and think of less attractive things and situations, things that have always worked in his dim and distant past, however, they did not work this time.

There he was, laid out on a settee, log burner intensely flaming away, with a beautiful Indian woman attending to his wound in a very attentive manner. By this time Jasmina had manoeuvred and had her back towards him, because she was leant forward it raised her bottom slightly. Cam could not take his eyes off it, the jogging bottoms had slightly slid down from her waist, due to them being too big, exposing the tops of her buttocks. It was obvious she had no underwear on. Her skin was a beautiful light brown colour and very smooth, without imperfection. Time passed but no matter how he tried to think of other things to distract his mind from Jasmina, he couldn't. He was now thinking of how it would feel to hold and kiss her. What am I doing, he asked himself? He then questioned his own integrity. She is a woman still grieving for her mother, he reminded himself. At this Jasmina finished cleaning his leg, she turned to face him and moved closer, she leant forward and gently kissed him on the cheek but whilst doing so dragged her hand up his body, with the tips of her fingers just making contact with his skin. The touch was so light, almost as if it was not in contact with him, but it was. Without stopping, her fingers travelled up his body to his chest. Her fingers only touched his body for a second or two, while she kissed his cheek, but it was a second or two that he would never forget.

"Does that feel better?" she asked him upon finishing the kiss, but still close enough that it was almost a whisper in his ear.

Initially he was unsure what she meant but soon realised she meant his leg. He was suspicious that Jasmina was deliberately teasing him.

"It feels fine. Thank you," he replied in a broken voice after clearing his throat.

As she stood up, she made eye contact with him for a short while, she had a knowing smile on her face, not one of teasing although it could easily have been interpreted as that, but one of understanding, acceptance and respect. A smile that he had not seen before.

"No," she said, as she made her way into the kitchen.

"I'm the one who should be thanking you," she added.

He was not sure why Jasmina should be thanking him, he thought that if she had known what he was thinking, she wouldn't be thanking him.

Cam knew he needed to go shopping for food but also knew that Jasmina would need some clothes and toiletries. Once his erection had passed he stood up from the settee.

"Do you fancy coming to the shops?" he asked Jasmina.

"Yes please, I need to get some things," she replied.

Cam decided to go against his principles and head for a large supermarket where they could get everything under one roof.

They both got showered and dressed, Cam made sure not to be in close proximity of Jasmina to save further embarrassment. Cam did the gentlemanly act of walking Colin whilst Jasmina showered, he knew that if he could hear her showering and smell the soap and shampoo, it would get his mind wandering again to thoughts of a sexual nature. They were thoughts that he knew he could not control, so therefore needed to avoid.

Cam detested shopping, but whilst travelling to the supermarket he felt comfortable, relaxed and without trepidation. A strange sensation indeed, what did this woman possess that could make him feel this way?

CHAPTER 7 THE BOND

"That was a great meal, I'm so full I can hardly move," Jasmina said as she and Cam entered the bungalow from the shopping trip. He always enjoyed entering his home, he felt like it was his cosy retreat from the world outside.

"Me too, I feel like I won't need to eat for a week. I don't think the beer has helped though, I know it's only a couple of pints but it still takes up room. I'll fire up the log burner and then I'll make a brew," Cam said as he placed the bags of shopping in the hallway.

Their shopping trip had been successful, they purchased enough food for both of them for a week or so, and Jasmina had purchased her much needed clothes and toiletries. As Cam is not a shopper, he organised their duties, Cam did the food shop whilst Jasmina shopped for her personal items. It appeared to have worked well, there was no conflict and they did it in half the time, allowing them to go for a rather large pub meal on their way home.

The log burner, to Cam's relief, was just about still burning so he just needed to put some logs on. He swiftly put the food shopping away and made the tea.

Cam collapsed onto the settee with his mug of tea. Jasmina took up her usual position in the armchair, nearest the heat source, and they both relaxed and watched the flames flicker and dance.

"I've been thinking," Cam said.

"The first thing we need to do is to confirm that your father is still alive, I know we think he is, but we need to confirm this. Once this is done we need to find out where he works, if he still does, or where he lives. I've searched all the possible sites on the internet but nothing has been identified, he is still shown as a director of the company at companies house but that could be out of date, also it doesn't show us a picture of him.

This means that I will go to The Allan Hotel and use my intuition to find out what I can. I have a few things in my shed that may help. Unfortunately, you will need to take a back seat as they may be looking for you. This means you have the important task of covering my back. I can't tell you how important that is, because this could get messy," he added.

"It sounds dangerous, you don't have to do it, you know. I don't want you getting hurt," Jasmina said.

"I should be fine, don't worry, just keep your eyes peeled. Sorry, that means stay alert," he said.

"I think we should go to London tomorrow and start the process. We can sleep in a bed and breakfast outside the city if we need to stay down there. Most bed and breakfasts are independent so there is no worry of it being part of their company. I have a spare mobile phone that you can have so we can stay in contact. Just make sure you don't get arrested," he added.

"It all sounds so complicated, I never expected it would all come to this," she said.

"Well it's what I used to do for a living don't forget. As a precaution, please leave the clothes here that you wore when we met, they have seen them and you'll be on CCTV in the hotel wearing them. You may also want to wear your hair in a different style," he said.

"Ok, anything you say," she said.

They both drank their mugs of tea and stared into the log burner thoughtfully. However, the heat and flames were working their magic and making them increasingly relaxed and sleepy.

"Do you want to see the clothes I bought?" Jasmina suddenly asked, breaking the silence.

"Yes, ok," replied Cam, in an enthusiastic manner, however he really wasn't bothered at all. Clothes were definitely not his thing. He stayed on the settee gazing in thought at the log burner.

"Well, what do you think?" Jasmina asked as she entered the room and turned on the main light.

Cam looked up and assessed her clothing, she wore a fluffy type pullover which was red in colour, and a pair of black tight leggings.

"Very nice," he said.

However, he didn't know whether he was remarking on the clothes or Jasmina herself. Her leggings clung to her very feminine figure, they showed a distinct outline of her calves, thighs, hips and bottom. Yet again, he felt like a naughty schoolboy, having no control over his emotions and not knowing where to look. He thought she looked beautiful and very, very sexy.

"Good. I'll show you the others," she said as she left the lounge.

Cam was hoping she would come back in some very unflattering clothing which wouldn't make him feel embarrassed.

"What about these?" she asked as she entered the room again.

"Very nice," he remarked again.

This time she wore a tight fitting white top, a short black skirt and black tights. Again the outfit left very little for his imagination regarding her figure. The tights again outlined her very shapely, firm legs. Cam could not take his eyes off her, he didn't want to stare but he couldn't help himself. The more he told himself not to look, the more he looked.

His mind was telling him to go and make a cup of tea, or do anything, but he couldn't. She turned off the light and began to walk towards him, he could feel himself getting hot, uncomfortable and sexually aroused. As she neared, he again could smell her sweet perfume. Upon reaching him she whispered in his ear,

"It's ok, it's what I want." She immediately placed her soft, full lips on his and they began to kiss. It was at this point that Cam knew things were ok for him to express his feelings. Without words, Cam kissed her back, creating an immediate feeling of electricity. He never knew a kiss could produce such feelings, both physical and emotional. He felt their lips had become a conduit of emotion, with each other's emotion being warmly accepted and understood by the receiver.

Jasmina pulled Cam to his feet, there they stood, two people completely absorbed by the other, as if the world around them didn't exist. They only had eyes for each other, interest in each other, and a deep desire for each other. Jasmina undid the buttons on Cam's shirt allowing it to fall to the floor and expose his manly, hairy chest, which she gently ran her hands over. Cam returned the compliment, his hands gently gliding over her breasts, he felt like his hands had never touched anything so perfect. He felt her breasts become more alive with every one of her deep breaths, and her nipples become erect. Jasmina undid his jeans and they too fell to the floor, Cam pulled Jasmina to him and held her tightly, he kissed her neck and gently caressed her back, he could feel her quiver and knew she was feeling the same way as him. He gazed into her big green eyes and, without words, told her how wonderful she was, this was reciprocated by Jasmina.

At this very moment, he thought she was the most wonderful thing he had ever seen or touched. He nervously removed Jasmina's new clothes. They both lay on the settee and began to passionately make love. The flames from the log burner provided a warm, flickering light, which Cam thought enhanced the colour and beauty of Jasmina's perfect skin. The flickering light continued to dance on Jasmina's skin, as though it was the dance of love.

She placed her hand behind his head and looked deep into his eyes, Cam looked deep into her eyes, they were both lost in each other's souls. He could feel the pleasure in Jasmina's body too by the way it was pushing towards him. They knew at that moment they had created a lifelong, unbreakable bond. It was a once in lifetime moment and they both knew it. Their lovemaking was passionate, sensitive, gentle and beautiful, a perfect fusion. At its conclusion they both lay there, exhausted, contented and relaxed.

"Are you ok?" he asked.

"Yes, are you?" she replied.

Cam was still in the moment of ecstasy and couldn't say any more, he just murmured with satisfaction.

With the log burner keeping them warm, they fell asleep in each other's arms with the knowledge that something very special indeed, had just occurred.

They slept for a couple of hours, holding each other tightly, like they were afraid to let go, and then Cam woke. He looked at Jasmina and couldn't believe how fortunate he was, lying there with a beautiful woman he had just made love with, log burner still flickering and providing heat and the smell of Jasmina's sweet perfume stimulating his nasal senses. At that moment he knew if he died, there and then, he would die the happiest man in the world. Whilst lost in his pleasant thoughts, Jasmina too woke up.

She looked in his eyes, smiled and said, "Hello."

"Hello," Cam replied with a warm smile on his face.

He was hoping that Jasmina didn't wake with the regret of what had happened between them, her smile went a long way to relieving him of his worry.

"I think we should go to bed and get some proper sleep," he suggested to Jasmina.

"Yes, let's do that," she replied.

Cam pulled on his boxers and made a brew whilst Jasmina got dressed for bed. After sorting Colin, Cam made his way to the bedroom with the mugs of tea. It had been a few years since Cam had shared his bed with a woman, but on seeing Jasmina already in bed, he felt as though it was just about the most natural thing ever. He placed the mug of tea on the cabinet, at her chosen side of the bed, this suited Cam because he was nearer the window and liked to sleep with it open. As he slid into bed, Cam felt the warmth of Jasmina's legs against his, she cuddled up right against him.

"Cam, I have a confession to make," she announced.

Cam's heart sank. I knew it was too good to be true, he thought, and prepared himself for bad news.

"I almost knew this moment would happen from the time we hugged in the cafe. I felt something special then, safe, comfortable, excited and happy all at the same time, even though I had no right to because I was still grieving for my mother. Something happened but I don't know what it was," she confessed.

"I know exactly what you mean, I felt it too," he replied.

"Since then, I have been testing my own instinct and your integrity. I wanted to know if that moment in the cafe was just a passing moment of vulnerability, but it wasn't, everything I felt then I still do, but with more intensity. I knew you found me attractive and I wanted to know if you were the type of man to bring a woman to a strange place and use her vulnerability to your own advantage. You certainly haven't done so, not at all, you have acted like a perfect gentleman, especially when I was cleaning your leg. I was teasing you then by placing my bottom towards you knowing that you would be looking at it. I knew you were sexually aroused, but you did well not to place your hand on me or make some sexual innuendo.

When you thanked me for cleaning your leg, I thanked you in return, and you looked at me in a quizzical way. I was thanking you for your perfect behaviour," she said.

Cam listened intently.

"As a waitress in Goa, I have been subject to many sexual innuendos, and unwanted hands being placed upon my body. Lots of wealthy European holiday-makers think that because they have paid for the use the hotel's facilities, they have paid to treat me like their little Indian toy. You are very different, you have treated me with respect and consideration. You have put my needs before your own without question, and expected nothing in return. I have never met a man like you before, I've only ever had two boyfriends before, one was an Indian boy when I was a teenager, he expected me to marry him and have children with him, and to become almost a slave to him.

The other was a European man who was working in Goa, it became apparent that he just wanted to have company and a good time whilst he was there. That was almost ten years ago, I've not been bothered since, those two experiences put me off men for life, that is until I met you.

You make me feel a way that's impossible to describe, but it's a wonderful feeling.

"Even when I was showing you my clothes in a seductive manner, you maintained your discipline and stayed sat down. In that position a lot of men would have pounced on me. You were man enough to let me take control and approach you, that was the final test.

As soon as you started to make love to me, I knew without doubt, that for me you are 'the one'. I truly believe that opportunity only comes once during a lifetime," Jasmina stated.

"I felt that too, at that moment I knew you were 'the one'," Cam said.

"My mother, according to my aunt, found 'the one', my father, but she unfortunately didn't have the opportunity to live with him. She raised me on her own, without help, she was a strong beautiful woman. I wish she could know how happy I feel right now. I'm sure she would be thrilled for me and proud of herself. She is the one who encouraged me to lose my strong accent, and speak English to a good standard, in the hope that I may travel. It's ironic that my need to travel is down to her death, perhaps she knew I would look for my father, what do you think?" Jasmina asked.

"It's certainly a possibility," replied Cam, who was totally engrossed in watching Jasmina talk. He watched every movement of her lips, felt every breath she took and almost felt every one of her heartbeats.

"You would have liked her, Cam, I know that she would have seen all the good in you and liked you very much," she said.

"Jasmina, I would never have taken advantage of you. I am twenty years older than you, why ever would I think that you would be interested in me? I have shut the world out due to life's trials and tribulations, I am not a moaner but I've had some hard times. I've seen enough death to last four lifetimes, worked all sorts of stupid long hours, suffered more stress than any human being should have to, and to top it all due to a divorce, three of my four children don't speak to me. That is why I don't hold myself in high esteem and can't be bothered with all the greed of life. I don't need much money and I don't need friends. The thought of my children not speaking to me breaks my heart every single day, and I don't think that will ever change.

So forgive me for being so shocked that a beautiful, young, amazing woman would be interested in me. I hope I don't disappoint you," Cam said.

At this, Jasmina snuggled her bottom into Cam's lap as though it was something she had been doing for years. Cam placed his arm over Jasmina and pulled her even closer to him. He held her tight so that she would feel safe and protected. He could feel her heart beating and smell her perfume. He went to sleep with the most perfect feeling. A perfect end to a perfect day, he thought.

CHAPTER 8 THE SEARCH

Cam and Jasmina set off early next morning, in his much trusted VW, to locate her father, They had packed clothes, food and some technical items to help in their quest. On the long journey they discussed the previous evening's events and how they saw their future together. They were both committed to giving their newly found romance the best chance they possibly could. They both knew that there was something very special between them. During the journey, they both took every opportunity to touch each other, whether that be a hand, leg, face or hair. Their desire for each other filled the car with the most positive and optimistic ambience. To Cam's surprise and delight, Jasmina had suggested that if they were successful in locating her father, and he acknowledged her, she would like to move to England to be with Cam and give herself a chance of getting to know her father. Delighted as Cam was with this news, he reiterated that there was no guarantee of finding her father, and if they did, no guarantee of him acknowledging Jasmina.

After what seemed to them like a day's travelling they reached the vicinity of The Allan Hotel. Cam found a suitable parking space that allowed Jasmina to stay in the car.

"Before we have a cup of tea, I'll go to the hotel and see what information I can find out, we can then have a cup of tea and discuss what further action to take, if any," Cam said.

"Ok," Jasmina replied.

There was an obvious air of apprehension, which was to be expected, Cam tried to reassure Jasmina that it should all be fine, It was easier for him due to having been in these situations many times before during his professional career. Cam, from the rear of the car, produced a letter addressed to Mr Thomas Allan, a motorcycle jacket and a motorcycle helmet with a camera fixed to it.

"This is what I used to use on my motorbike. The camera can record whatever I am looking at. The letter has my phone number in it so your father can call it, should I get the letter to him," he said.

Jasmina's face suddenly became very serious with a look of concern, as though the whole situation had become very real, and not just an idea. Cam gave Jasmina a reassuring look and kissed her gently on the cheek as he got out of the car.

"Wish me luck. I shouldn't be any longer than fifteen minutes," he said.

Off he walked with letter and helmet in hand as Jasmina looked on nervously. She found it hard to sit still, she kept rubbing her hands and looking at the clock to see how many more seconds had passed, she really wanted Cam back in her arms, safe and well.

Just prior to The Allan Hotel, Cam found a suitably quiet location and popped on his motorbike helmet and jacket. The full face helmet had a dark visor which really hid his face, he switched the camera on and made his way to the hotel doors. The doors were automatically operated, as they opened he got his first glimpse of the very impressive reception area. It was how Jasmina had described it, including the glass office which overlooked the whole area. Prior to going to the desk, Cam went and looked at the opposite wall. There, to his satisfaction, were numerous photographs displayed of the hotel employees, a sort of who's who. He had a good long look to see if Jasmina's father was there, but he wasn't, the top photograph, of the pyramid shape, was a female. Her name was Laura Allan, she appeared to be about thirty years old with an unblemished face, potentially due to the heavy but perfect makeup she was wearing, perfectly straightened hair which appeared to be almost black in colour, not wearing a smile but a very serious pout. She was just the type of person Cam disliked.

"Can I help you, sir?" came the question from the woman behind the reception desk.

As Cam made his way towards the desk he looked up at the elevated glass office situated directly behind the desk, in the office he clearly saw the woman, he now knows as Laura Allan. She looks as unfriendly in the flesh as she does in her photo, he thought to himself.

"I have a letter for Mr Thomas Allan that he needs to sign for," he said.

He saw Laura Allan immediately get to her feet and direct her attention towards him. He realised that she was going to make her way down towards him, so he knew he had to get any information, from the receptionist, as quickly as possible.

"Well is he here? I haven't got all day!" he said abruptly.

"Mr Allan doesn't..." the receptionist began to say before being aggressively interrupted by Laura Allan.

"Can I help you?" she said in a somewhat patronising manner.

Cam didn't want to look as though he was interested in Laura Allan so only really glanced in her direction. He could see that she was dressed in a very smart, expensive trouser suit which was black in colour.

Due to what the receptionist started to say, Cam knew that Thomas Allan wasn't at the hotel and that he probably didn't work there anymore. He immediately detected a cold ruthlessness about Laura Allan, this made it easier for him to be decisive in his own actions towards her.

"I have a letter for Mr Thomas Allan that needs to be signed for. Could you tell me if he is here?" Cam said.

"He's not available to sign for it at this moment, I'll sign for it," Laura Allan said, as though she would be doing him a huge favour.

"This is my first day on this job so I can't risk anybody else signing for it. I don't want the sack. If he's not here and if it's not too far, I can take it to his house," Cam stated.

Laura Allan looked at Cam as though he was a piece of dirt that was clinging to the bottom of her new shoes. Cam thought she had a look that could freeze hell and definitely scare even the bravest of children.

"Let's get this straight, shall we? If you think I'm going to give you the personal address of my father, you are sadly mistaken. You either let me sign for it or you can take it back!" she said sternly.

This statement was good news for Cam because he couldn't let Laura Allan have the information contained in the letter, inadvertently she had just made his exit from the hotel very easy.

"Yes, madam, as you wish," Cam replied, in an ever so slightly sarcastic manner, he just couldn't help himself.

Cam left the hotel as quickly as he could and started to make his way back to Jasmina, hoping that she was ok.

On his journey he thought about Laura Allan, and how she was one-dimensional, ambitious, greedy, unforgiving, inconsiderate and many more unflattering things. She had certainly earned herself a place in the top ten list of the most arrogant people he had ever met. Cam often questioned his instincts and gut reactions to things and people. He often proved himself to be correct, however, on this occasion the need to question himself did not even cross his mind. He wondered how he could break the news to Jasmina, that not only did she have a sister like Laura Allan who he thought was a poor specimen of a human being, but the fact that he was now convinced that Laura Allan was somehow connected to Jasmina being followed.

On his arrival back at the car, the smile on Jasmina's face filled him with joy.

"I'm so glad you're safe," she said, just prior to hugging him and kissing him.

Cam was thrilled with his reception.

"I'm glad that you're safe too. I need a cup of tea, I'm sure you do too," he said.

They headed off, hand in hand, and found a cafe at the rear of a superstore. Not perfect, Cam thought, but they managed to find some seats in an alcove which afforded them some privacy.

Cam explained in detail what had happened at the hotel, and of his thoughts about Laura Allen. Jasmina took a few minutes to digest the information.

"Why would a sister do that to her sister?" she asked.

"I can only assume that it's greed or jealousy, or that somebody is trying to keep you a secret. We can't say for definite who, it could be your father. We are not actually sure that they know you are his daughter, how could they?" he asked.

"I don't know, I'm confused about how people can behave like this. I just wanted to tell my father that my mother had died," she said.

"Let's not make too many assumptions and try to stick to the facts and what we do know. We now know that your father is alive. Surely that is good news?" Cam said.

"Yes it is. Yes it is, Cam," Jasmina said in a resilient manner.

Cam took the memory card from his helmet camera and placed it in his phone, they both watched as he played the recording. It didn't show them anything that they didn't know already but it confirmed their immense dislike of Laura Allan. On listening to the conversation between her and Cam, Jasmina became more positive about the fact that her father appeared to be alive.

"What we need to do now is locate him," Cam said.

"Yes, but how?" Jasmina replied with an air of desperation about her.

"I plan to hide in the hotel car park and wait for Laura to finish work. When she goes to her car, I'll know what car she drives. I'm sure she'll park there because parking spaces are hard to find in London, as you've seen. Once I know what car she drives I can attach a GPS tracking device to it, this will tell us where the car goes and hopefully she'll go to your father's house. The device is one that I used on my motorbike in case it was ever stolen - it was once, and I found it within hours. I took photos of it and told the police where it was, luckily I got it back with very little damage to it. Lots of people have them on their vehicles, it just means that my tracker will be on someone else's car. This is it," he said.

Cam pulled from his pocket a small black box and showed it to Jasmina, she looked at it with a very disbelieving expression on her face. He put his arm around her, not only for reassurance, but also to remind her how much he cared. She responded with a smile and affectionately kissed his cheek. He knew that this was a very emotional time for her, not only because of the search for her father but also because of their emotions for each other.

They walked back towards the car, Cam could feel the tension in her hand as he held it.

"I feel sick with worry, Cam. I have a feeling that something horrible is going to happen, but I don't know what. We can stop looking if you want, it'll be ok, at least we would have tried," she said.

"It'll be fine. We've come this far and done so much, it would be a shame if we didn't do what we set out to do," he said.

At this they stopped and hugged each other, that same magical feeling happened where the rest of the world didn't matter, they were absolutely right for each other.

They relocated his trusted VW to a less prominent parking space as Cam didn't know how long he would need to be hidden in the car park. It was 3pm and getting dark.

"I don't know what time Laura will finish work and I don't want to miss her, so I'm going now. My phone will be on silent but if you need me just ring, if I don't answer please don't worry, it just means that there are people about, after all it is a hotel car park. If I phone you asking if you have found him, just bring the dog lead into the car park and I'll do the talking. We'll pretend that we have lost our dog," he said whilst handing a dog lead to Jasmina.

Cam dressed himself in the warmest, darkest clothing he had, with a black woollen hat pulled down to just above his eyes. His coat was his old motorbike jacket which had seen lots of use and better days, but it was still warm and waterproof.

"Not a pretty sight, I know, but at least I'll be warm. I'll be back before you know it," he said as he left the car.

Within minutes Cam had positioned himself behind the hotel bins at the rear of the car park. He could smell old rotting food, and see the resident hotel car park rats, he watched them scurry around the bins area, some were the size of domestic cats. He then realised that the moisture soaking into his trousers from the floor probably contained other contaminants, not just clean rainwater.

From his position he could see the whole of the car park. He settled himself in a comfortable position and assessed the cars on the car park, trying to guess which one was Laura's car. With the opinion that most people's cars have a reflection on some of their character traits, as his own car did. It didn't take him long to choose what car he thought matched Laura's personality. It was a white Audi A8, the brightest cleanest white imaginable. Cam was not too interested in cars because he thought that most modern cars lacked character, but he knew that this Audi had a three litre turbocharged engine which produced well over three hundred horse power, about seven times more than his trusted VW. 'Just what's needed to negotiate the traffic in a city,' he thought sarcastically. The Audi was big and took up two parking spaces. It had gleaming five-spoke alloy wheels, of which one alone was probably worth more than his car. He thought that it was definitely the type of car you would have if you wanted to be noticed, or wanted your wealth to be noticed. He had an idea it would be worth around £75,000. It saddened him when he thought of the worthwhile things that substantial amount of money could be spent on.

As he sat and waited his mind drifted to Jasmina, and he felt wonderful inside. He thought of how fortunate he was to experience such feelings of joy when he had 'given up' on daring to even think of such happiness. He truly believed that she was, not only the most wonderful woman he had ever met, but also beginning to show that she was, emotionally, the deepest woman he had ever met.

The weather worsened, it was now wet, cold and dark. Cam heard the sound of a large diesel engine approaching, he then saw it was a bin lorry, coming to empty the bins, the ones he was hiding behind. He could not risk being seen, he knew that the car park would be covered by CCTV. He quickly rolled underneath the nearest parked vehicle, luckily for him it was a four wheel drive which was high off the ground. The lorry backed up to the bins and the men jumped from the cab. Cam could see their feet, hear them talking and smell the stench coming from the bin lorry.

"I see that bitch has got another new car. There was nothing wrong with the other one," said the first one.

"I know, the workers in there are probably on minimum wage and she's showing off in that. It's probably worth more than my flat," said the second one.

"Do you know her dad used to give us a good tip at Christmas? But if it's the same as last year we'll get sod all off her," said the first one, answering his own question.

"Yes, it's a shame he retired but I can see why. Would you want to be stuck in an office with that sour face all day?" asked the second one.

"No thanks, I would rather earn what I earn, smell like I do and be able to say what I want, when I want, rather than be bullied by her," said the first one.

They subsequently emptied the bins and left the car park, unfortunately for Cam the bins were left in a different position which wasn't conducive for him viewing the car park. Time was passing and he had to make a decision as to where to move. He decided that he would gamble and get as close to the Audi as possible. He crawled along the floor taking cover under vehicles that were high enough for him to do so. Hotel workers and guests were walking to and from their cars. He didn't want to be seen, it could result in him being beaten up, arrested or both. He eventually got to the car parked directly behind the Audi, he crawled underneath it and could see the registration plate on the Audi, it read, LIIURA, which confirmed it was her car. Cam very much disliked people who felt the need to pronounce their name to the world by means of displaying registration plates illegally. Cam crawled forward underneath the car, towards the Audi, at this he heard the footsteps of what he would describe as stiletto footsteps. He was right, he saw a pair of feet in stiletto style shoes walking towards the Audi, he assumed it was Laura Allan, the shoes looked very expensive indeed. They had heels of about three inches, about a size six or seven and were made from what appeared to be very soft leather, albeit bright red in colour. Cam didn't recognise the shoes because he didn't look at her feet when he met her earlier. The Audi door opened, Cam wasn't in position to put the tracker on the car, the Audi started up and he heard it click into gear, the engine revved and it began to move forward. He could feel that all of his planning had been a waste of time and that he was going to let Jasmina down. He knew he couldn't do this to her, it would break her heart. Out of complete desperation he just stretched his arm out with the tracker in it hoping it would make contact with the Audi. To his surprise and considerable discomfort, it did, pulling his arm in a most awkward direction, he lay there in pain for a short time, wondering if the tracker had actually stuck to the car or not.

Still making sure he wasn't seen, he crawled from under the car and made his way back to Jasmina.

On his arrival at his trusted VW, Jasmina again gave him the biggest, warmest smile he ever could have imagined. His heart was full of joy again. It was obvious she was very pleased to see him.

"Are you ok?" he asked her.

"Yes, I'm better now that I know you're safe," she replied.

At this, they kissed and hugged as though they hadn't seen each other for years, not the couple of hours or so that Cam had spent in the car park. They found it a struggle being apart from each other, even for the smallest amount of time.

Cam informed Jasmina of what he had done. He started the engine to warm them both, Jasmina was cold from being sat still without any heat source.

"If the tracker has stuck on the car and is working ok, I should get a signal on my phone. It will tell us where the vehicle is, there is a slight delay on it so we won't know where it is every second," he said.

It appeared like it was working he had a signal that was showing the location of the tracker. The signal showed where the tracker was on a map. It wasn't perfectly accurate but it would hopefully give them some idea of where Jasmina's father lived.

"I think it's time for something to eat and a well-earned cup of tea," he said.

"That would be lovely. I need the loo too," she replied.

They found the nearest pub that did food and eagerly entered it. They ordered their food and drinks and found a table. Jasmina went off to the toilets and Cam checked for an update on the tracker. It showed it was heading in the direction of Surrey, this made sense to Cam because he knew that parts of it were very affluent. Jasmina returned and removed her coat, as she warmed up she began to relax a little and the sparkle returned to her large green eyes. Cam had already removed his old motorbike jacket, it was far too warm to wear indoors.

Their food arrived, quicker than they anticipated, and they eagerly tucked in. Both had a vegetable curry, and whilst eating his, Cam pondered about Jasmina's culinary skills.

"Do you cook curries?" he asked in an inquisitive manner.

"Yes I do, they are a lot different to this one we're eating though. I don't know any Indian women who can't cook a curry," she replied.

Cam then mentally got lost in wondering what Jasmina's curries tasted like.

"Do you cook curries?" she asked Cam.

"I do but I do it the lazy way, from a jar." he replied.

He could see a tiny smile develop on Jasmina's face, as though she was thinking, typical man.

On finishing their food, Cam checked his phone. He could have sat there for ages, just talking to and enjoying the company of Jasmina, but he knew that the tracker had a short battery life and they had to make use of it.

"Write this address down," he said eagerly to Jasmina.

"The car has stopped, this could be it, this could be your father's address," he added excitedly.

Jasmina wrote the address down.

"It's about a fifty minute drive from here, shall we get going?" he asked.

Jasmina's face lit up and her eyes widened, just like a child on Christmas morning.

"Yes, let's go now," she replied.

They hurried back to the trusted VW and without hesitation set off towards Surrey. During the journey Jasmina said very little. It was clear to Cam that she was considering how she would feel on meeting her father, and probably wondering what she would say to him. He also understood that her considerations were possibly bringing back some memories of her mother. He let her be alone with her thoughts.

After just over an hour's travelling, Cam was relieved to be out of the city now, they arrived close to the destination where the tracker had indicated the vehicle had stopped. Not wanting to expose Jasmina to any kind of stress or conflict, he left her in the car whilst he made his way on foot and parked a few hundred yards away. As he neared the destination, he could clearly see that it was not a residential area; it was actually a trendy gym and spa. He was a little disappointed about this, but happy the tracker worked. He searched the car parks but found no trace of the Audi then subsequently made his way back to Jasmina.

On reaching Jasmina, she once again produced that smile which welcomed his return. He wondered how he had ever lived without it, he also answered his own question, unhappily.

He informed Jasmina of his finding and immediately looked on his phone to see if there had been any further movement of the tracker, to his pleasure and surprise there had been. It was now showing a location about ten miles from their present location. As they set off it was obvious to each other that they were both really excited. They didn't talk too much but they were both thinking that this could be it, this could actually be the home of her father. As they reached the location, they both looked questioningly at each other, they had travelled to a more rural location, all they could see in the immediate vicinity were bare trees, leaves on the ground and a narrow country lane. Cam stopped the car, their anticipation and excitement had turned to confusion and despair.

"What's happened, Cam? Why has it brought us here?" Jasmina asked.

"I'm not sure, I can only assume that because I didn't put the tracker on correctly, as I would have liked to have done, it's either fallen off or the battery is dead. Jasmina, I'm so sorry, I feel like I've let you down and that's something I never wanted to do," he replied.

They both sat there, in darkness, in the rain and deep into the countryside, disappointingly contemplating their lack of progress. This was the first moment that any potential stress between them could have reared its ugly head, but it didn't.

"Don't worry, Cam, perhaps it wasn't meant to be," she said.

Cam could hear the disappointment and resignation in her voice about not finding her father. He felt heartbroken for her, all the optimism and energy he had once witnessed, had gone.

"I need a wee," Cam said as he exited the car.

He walked off into the woods to find a suitable spot. Jasmina sat there, alone, getting cold, in a strange place, in a strange country. The quietness gave her time to think of her mother. Due to the activity in the city, her mind had been focused elsewhere. The thoughts of her mother took her back to happy times in Goa, in the warmth and sunshine. She could feel the love of her mother and see her wonderful smile. As Cam had felt like he had let Jasmina down, she in turn felt like she had let her mother down.

After ten or fifteen minutes had passed, she felt concerned for Cam and wondered if he had got lost in the dark, or been taken ill. She began to panic, she couldn't drive and although she didn't know where she was, she knew that she was miles from anywhere.

"Jasmina," Cam said loudly and excitedly, making her jump.

"I've found the car, the Audi, it's about three hundred yards over there behind those trees. I'd recognise that monstrosity of a car anywhere. The house is huge and has alarms and cameras everywhere. I reckon the tracker dropped off here but it did its job. That could be your father's house," he added.

Jasmina looked at Cam, he had a huge smile on his face and was once again full of energy. This in turn dramatically lifted her mood, it was as though they could feel each other's happiness and sadness. Cam could see the sparkle return to her large green eyes, and feel the return of her optimism.

"Come on, let's go!" Jasmina said in an overexcited voice.

"No, we can't. We haven't planned, and if it's not, we could blow the whole thing. We don't know who's there, if we knock on the door and your father isn't there, Laura Allan will know that you are still in the country. That is our trump card, her not knowing. Tomorrow we need to find out exactly who is in the house. I don't know how yet but I'll find a way," he said.

Reluctantly, Jasmina agreed with Cam. She knew he was right and trusted him, without question. She couldn't believe that in a matter of minutes, her emotions had gone from feeling full of anticipation and excitement, to feelings of despair, and now back to being full of anticipation and excitement.

That evening they found a bed and breakfast, not too far from where they had located the Audi. It was an old-fashioned and rural pub, The Nag's Head. The room was basic but comfortable with tea making facilities, for which they were most grateful and subsequently made the most of. With their thirst quenched and their bodies warmed, they went to bed exhausted from the day's events, the rollercoaster of emotions had certainly taken its toll on them. In bed they clung onto each other as though it was a case of life or death, they could be described as inseparable. Although they had not disclosed their love for each other, they both felt their love was all consuming, and without question. Cam fell asleep, not only with his heart full of love and contentment, but with his nasal senses full of Jasmina's sweet perfume.

CHAPTER 9 THE QUESTION

The following morning, Jasmina woke refreshed, warm and comfortable but with a feeling something wasn't quite right. She lay there, with her senses slowly coming to life, trying to fathom out the niggling feeling she had. She stretched her leg across the bed, still with her eyes closed, to feel Cam's flesh against hers, but to her dismay all she felt was the coldness of an empty space and bed sheets. She immediately turned over to find that he wasn't there, he must be in the shower, she thought. She called his name a few times but got no reply. Reluctantly, she got out of the warm and comfortable bed and searched the bathroom. Cam was not there, a feeling of panic fell upon her, she feared that he had left her and that she may never see him again.

"I asked too much of him," she muttered to herself.

"Why should I have expected him to do all this for me?" she asked herself as she continued to mutter.

"Why should I have expected him to be any different from any other man?" she questioningly muttered to herself in an attempt not to feel disappointed.

She sat there for a few minutes in despair, again she found herself pondering her fate in a foreign country with no friends and nobody to ask for help. Her mood again had gone from such positivity to deepest negativity. Almost by habit, as she had acquired a real desire for tea, she went to the kettle to make a brew. There, strategically placed in the handle of the kettle, was a note, she hastily grabbed it and, expecting the worst news possible, began to read it.

My darling Jasmina. I'm so sorry I'm not there to greet your awakening with a kiss and a cuddle, but if I'm to find out who lives in the house, I needed to leave early. You looked so beautiful and peaceful whilst you were sleeping that it would have been a shame to wake you. Don't worry about me, I'll be fine, I have put your phone on charge so I will call you when I have news. If I'm not back by the time you need to vacate the room, please stay in the pub. We can't risk you being seen. I have left enough money on the side so you can get food etc. I hope this ok. I love and miss you, and know that I'm yours forever. Cam.

On reading the note, Jasmina started to cry, they weren't tears of sadness but of joy. Her heart felt full again, for the first time since her mother had died, so full that it felt like it was going to burst out of her chest. It was the first time Cam had ever mentioned the word love to her, let alone tell her that he actually loved her. She was thrilled because her feelings towards him were being reciprocated. She wanted to scream and tell the world how much she was in love with a most fantastic, caring man. The thought of spending her life with him warmed her soul, just like sitting in her favourite chair, directly in front of a blazing log burner.

The two most important people that she wanted to tell about the way she felt were, firstly Cam, but she knew that she could not contact him because of the situation he was in. Secondly, her mother, she really would have loved to have had the conversation with her. She could explain how he makes her feel, and how he looks after and cares for her. She again realised how much she missed her mother, and how cruel fate had been to her with mother dying at such an early age. It would have been so easy to dwell on the sadness but the thought of Cam's love stopped her becoming melancholic. She adjusted her thought process back to positivity and waited for the safe return of her lover.

Cam had written the note several hours earlier prior to leaving the room. He had not considered the impact of what he had written but had just done it because it felt natural and was the truth.

He had made his way to the large house that he had seen the previous evening, where the white Audi was parked. He chose to watch from a position situated about five yards short of the very impressive electric gates. From here he had a good view of people and vehicles entering and exiting the house, providing him with the opportunity to identify them.

Cam's impression of the house was that, it was relatively new, almost a mock Tudor style, probably five or six bedroomed, double garage, which stood on a very substantial plot indeed and was worth a few million pounds.

Due to him being so close to the gates, the only way of concealment was to dig himself a hole, and then cover himself with the abundance of leaves that lay on the ground. As he lay in the damp soil, keeping the worms company, he imagined what the reaction of Thomas Allan would be, should he be fortunate enough to locate him. Cam looked at the house, its wealth and the potential type of person who would want to live that way, let alone be able to afford to live that way. Would he be of the same ilk as Laura Allan? Would he be in complete denial of Jasmina's mother? Would he just call the police and have me arrested, Cam asked himself? The more he thought about it, the more he convinced himself that Jasmina's existence would be denied or at least, a very bad memory that he had forgotten about. The more he convinced himself of this, the more he questioned the morality of his quest, not because he was concerned about upsetting Thomas Allan, but the woman he loved.

As the hours passed it began to get lighter, enough for Cam to identify whoever entered or exited the gates. Cam heard a diesel engine in the distance and knew it was coming his way, there was no other property around for what seemed like miles. The sound of the engine neared, and as it pulled adjacent to Cam, he could see it was a delivery van from one of the big online commerce companies. The driver, due to the position of the intercom system, exited his cab and informed the occupiers of his business there. Cam assumed the system was located there so that, the driver had no option but to exit the vehicle, in order that the camera could get a full image of whoever wanted to enter. The van entered and subsequently left approximately five minutes later. After that brief burst of activity it all went quiet again, Cam was left in his damp hole, alone with his thoughts.

An hour or so passed without movement or incident, but just as his spirits began to sag, he heard an engine fire into life. Cam's heart began to race and adrenaline pumped through his body. Was this it, the moment he'd waited hours for, confirmation that the Audi belonged to Laura Allan? He recognised the engine and exhaust note to be that of the Audi, after all, he had only been a few feet away from it the last time he heard it. As the Audi came into his view, due to being in the middle of the countryside, he thought it was very ostentatious and unfitting of the surroundings. The Audi neared the gates, it slowed but did not need to stop because the gates would have been electronically opened from within the car. It proceeded through the gates and as it drew level with Cam, he recognised a face he would never forget, that of Laura Allan. She again appeared of a stern disposition, had perfect hair and makeup and appeared to have on her mind, one thing and one thing only, herself.

The Audi roared off into the distance, with Laura Allan making use of its three hundred horse power. Cam became deep in thought about his next step, he was aware that his objective had been achieved, identifying that Laura Allan lived there, he was aware that his next step should be to regroup with Jasmina and plan their next move methodically. After all, the next move could possibly bring them into contact with Thomas Allan.

Whilst deep in thought, another delivery arrived at the gates, the vehicle was a good sized lorry with large doors at the rear. There was a step at the rear which aided access to the cargo area. The driver exited the cab, and just like the previous delivery driver had, went to the intercom. Whilst the driver was there Cam, who was out of sight of the driver and camera, instinctively climbed onto the rear step of the lorry. Once on it he immediately questioned his actions, he considered getting off but it was too late, the lorry was on the move. Once inside the gates, the lorry manoeuvred towards the house, Cam began to sweat a little, his heartbeat increased, his mouth went dry, if he stayed on the step he would, without doubt, be found and probably arrested on suspicion of burglary or some other criminal offence. He saw his opportunity.

Parked immediately outside the garage was a black Range Rover that he had not seen this from outside the gates, he jumped from the back of the lorry and rolled underneath it. With his heart pumping and the fear of being arrested, he almost froze to the spot. From his position on the floor he saw the lorry stop, and the driver jump from the cab and head towards the door of the house.

After a few seconds he heard voices, then after another few seconds had passed he saw the driver and another man emerge from the direction of the house and walk towards the back of the lorry. Cam could see the other man was older looking, about sixty-five years old, white skinned, short grey hair, approximately five feet ten inches in height, medium build and well-spoken but with a slightly stern accent. He wore a beige cardigan over a white shirt, brown chino trousers and brown brogue shoes. His attire certainly gave the impression that he was a wealthy man.

The driver and older man lifted a box from the lorry and walked towards the garage, right where Cam was hiding. He could hear them talking as they neared him, due to them being so close, all Cam could see was their feet. They stopped at the garage.

"Put it there," the older man said.

"Ok," replied the driver.

Cam was almost holding his breath, he was sure he was going to get found. He was sweating with fear, not because of what would happen to him so much, but because of Jasmina being left alone for so long if he were to be arrested, he knew she would be scared and lonely.

"That's a beautiful car," said the driver.

"It's ok, but at the end of the day, a car is a car," replied the older man.

Even in his situation, on hearing this, Cam found he had a liking of the older man's attitude.

"Sit in if you want, if you're that interested," said the older man.

This is not what Cam wanted to hear, if the car started he would either have to expose himself or risk getting injured. Cam heard the car doors unlock, his heart was racing so much he thought that they might actually hear it. The car rocked a little and sank on its suspension slightly, signalling to Cam that somebody had got into it. He decided to play safe and crawl out rather than risk getting injured. As he commenced to do it he heard voices again.

"It's really lovely," said the driver.

"Must be lovely to have leather seats."

The car then lifted a little, Cam knew the car was empty again. He then saw both men walk off towards the house. The driver jumped into his cab and the older man walked towards the door to the house. Cam was very relieved, he began to breathe again and his heart rate slowed to somewhere near normal.

"Goodbye, Mr Allan," the driver said.

Cam, who for a good few minutes due to thinking of his own safety, had completely forgotten why he was there. It's him, he thought to himself! It's him!! Thomas Allan.

He laid under the Range Rover for what seemed like an age, regaining his composure and wondering what to say to Thomas Allan. Reminding himself that the love of his life, Jasmina, was his reason for doing this. He summoned up the courage to crawl from beneath the sanctuary of the car and approach the front door. He was fully aware that what he was about to do could change people's lives forever, he knew not, if it would be for the better, or worse.

During his walk to the front door he could feel the tension in his whole body, his legs felt like they just did not want to work. The walk was a matter of yards, but to Cam, it felt like every yard was a mile. It was the muscle tension that can be caused by fear or apprehension that impacted on him greatly.

He reached the front door, it was a very impressive panelled hardwood door, painted black. Cam could see his reflection, it did not bode well he suspected, on realising that he actually looked like a man who'd been lying in a hole in the ground for hours, followed by ten minutes under a car. His bike jacket was filthy and his jeans looked like they needed to be, not washed, but thrown away. An ironic smile came to Cam's face as he thought to himself, I'm here for a meeting of such importance looking like this.

He rang the doorbell, it was so loud it sounded like Big Ben. The door slowly opened and Cam was presented with the older man, he had a look on his face that was shocked, angry and very stern. His face displayed the evidence of him having once been a very handsome man, however, it was apparent that he had worked hard during his life, not manual work but stressful work. It was well proportioned, his nose was manly but not too big, his mouth was still shaped, not sagging like some older people get, he was clean shaven, his ears were in proportion to his head and he had blue eyes. He was definitely the man in the photo that Jasmina had showed him.

"How did you get in and what do you want?" asked the older man.

"Excuse me for intruding, but I'm looking for Thomas Allan," Cam replied.

"You have no right to be here. If you don't leave I'm calling the police. I'm very good friends with the Superintendent," bellowed the older man.

"I'm so sorry to bother you, please let me explain," Cam replied.

"Explain what? Why you are trespassing?" asked the older man.

"Please don't call the police. I'm not here to cause trouble," Cam said.

"You should have thought about that before you broke into my grounds," the older man stated.

At this he produced a mobile phone and started to make a call. It was at that moment Cam became suspicious that Thomas Allan was behind the whole plot to scare Jasmina away. With this thought, Cam's whole demeanour changed from one of being defensive, to one of being offensive. He thought that if he was going to be arrested, at least he would have his say.

"Well, sir, shame on you for not wanting to listen to what I have to say. I am no thief, or burglar, just because I'm not wearing expensive clothes such as yourself, it is wrong to question my morality and lawfulness, especially when you know nothing about me. I have been polite to you and not raised my voice once, this respect has not been reciprocated. Your wealth and standing does not give you the right to treat people like that, you simply cannot bully people and scare people just to get what you desire. You may well own a chain of hotels and leisure centres, but may I inform you that you don't own me, and may I inform you, you never will. It's taken me so much effort to be here, to tell you something that may improve your life, but it appears you know what I have to say and you're obviously not interested," Cam said in a protesting manner.

"You could not possibly have anything to say that could be of interest to me," said the older man.

"You rude man. I feel sorry for you. There must be so much that you have missed out on in your life due to you not having the courtesy to listen," Cam said angrily. He had given it his best shot and blown it, rudeness was one thing that he always responded to negatively. He felt gutted for Jasmina, not only because it appeared she'd never meet her father, but also because he was a rude arrogant man. He suspected that this was where Laura Allan inherited her attitude from. As Cam walked away he turned and said to the older man,

"Whatever did Miss Singh see in you?"

Cam saw that this question stopped the older man in his tracks. He immediately cancelled the phone call and put the phone back in his pocket.

"What did you say?" he asked Cam in a soft quiet voice.

"'Whatever did Miss Singh see in you' is what I asked," Cam said, still angry with the older man.

"What do you know of Miss Singh?" asked the older man.

"Why should I tell you?" Cam asked in stubborn childish manner.

"I don't know who you are."

"I am Thomas Allan," said the older man. His demeanour had completely changed from a resilient, cold man to a well-mannered, warm man.-

"Well I'm Cameron Grant," Cam introduced himself.

"Cameron, won't you please come in?" asked Thomas Allan.

"Thank you, Mr Allan," Cam replied as he followed Thomas Allan into his home.

"Please call me Tom, Mr Allan is too formal," Tom said.

"Please call me Cam then," he said returning the compliment.

Once inside, Cam did what he was taught to do as a boy, remove his footwear, it didn't feel natural for him to parade around someone's home in dirty boots, he respected that they had probably worked very hard for what they owned. Whilst removing his boots, he naturally scanned the home of Thomas Allan.

The house, as expected, was very grand indeed. In the hallway where he stood, Cam could see a dining room to his right, it had a very large dining table in its centre, which was already laid with fine cutlery. To his left was a lounge, this had a three-piece suite that was huge, the settee alone wouldn't fit into Cam's lounge. It was made of leather and was cream in colour, on the far wall hung a tv, this again wouldn't fit into Cam's lounge. It appeared that all the rooms in the house were of very generous proportions. There was a cloakroom right next to the front door, at the rear of the hallway was the kitchen, from what Cam could see it was ultra-modern. The units were of a shiny gloss finish and dark grey in colour, the wall tiles were many different colours. Right in the middle of the hallway was a magnificent oak staircase. It spiralled as it went up, the steps on it were also made from oak and at least four feet wide. All the floors that Cam could see were made from oak, not an oak finish but solid oak. The house just oozed wealth and quality.

"Come and sit in the lounge, Cam, I'll make some tea," Tom said.

"That would be great," Cam replied.

As Cam became more relaxed, he gradually sank deeper and deeper into the leather settee, it was certainly large enough to have a comfortable sleep on.

Tom entered the room with the tea, not just two mugs of tea but a tray full of paraphernalia consisting of a beautiful china teapot, two matching cups with saucers, a silver pot of sugar with a silver spoon in it, two silver spoons on the saucers, a silver tea strainer with silver pot and a china plate full of assorted biscuits. Cam felt like he was having afternoon tea at the Ritz, not a brew with a man he had just met. The time it had taken Tom to make the tea had allowed both men to calm down and address each other appropriately.

"Cam, please tell me what you know about Miss Singh," Tom asked.

"Well, Tom, all I know is that you and her became acquainted thirty-odd years ago, whilst in Goa. I know that you came back to England when your business trip ended," Cam replied.

Tom became thoughtful and silent for a few seconds, as though his mind had wandered back to that time in Goa. At first he stared towards the window and then closed his eyes. Cam could see a serenity had fallen upon Tom. He waited, knowing that Tom was making the most of that moment, it was obvious by the expression on his face, it had changed from a frown of concern to a slight smile of contentment.

Tom's reaction was so spontaneous and honest, it was at that moment, Cam knew of the love that Tom once had for Jasmina's mother.

Tom opened his eyes and once again focused on Cam and the matter in hand.

"There is someone from Goa who is here to see you," Cam said.

"Who is it? Is it Sunita?" asked Tom in an excited manner.

"I'm sorry, Tom, I don't know who Sunita is," he replied.

"Sunita Singh, she worked, or still works there for all I know, at the Hotel Jasmin," Tom explained, his voice was now soft and gentle, almost apologetic.

Cam at that point realised that he'd never known or asked the first name of Jasmina's mother.

"Ok, Tom, That I never knew. There is not a lot more that I feel permitted to tell you. That's what this person has come all the way from Goa to do. If I say something I may give the wrong impression about stuff and it just may all get misinterpreted. I would hate to do that, especially after all the hard work that's gone into finding you. I think the best solution is for the two of you meet. Then all the questions that need to be asked and answered, can be, without any wrong information being passed. The question is, Tom, and it is a big question, are you prepared to meet them?" asked Cam

"How do I know that you're not trying to set me up with some sort of blackmail or robbery?" Tom asked in a slightly defensive manner.

"You don't, Tom. I hope you'll find it within you to trust me," Cam said.

"If I meet you, it needs to be away from here. I don't want my family knowing anything about it. You can understand why I am a little sceptical?" Tom asked.

"Yes I understand," Cam replied.

"There's a pub about ten miles or so from here called The Pheasant. I'll meet you there tomorrow at midday. I warn you, though, if I suspect anything that's the slightest bit underhand, I'll call the police straightaway. I'm not an easy man to convince, I warn you," Tom said.

Tom gave Cam the address of the pub. Cam was finishing his tea and biscuits, due to his early start and lack of breakfast, they tasted like the best he'd ever had.

"Here's my phone number, Tom, if you change your mind or you can't make it, would you please let me know?" Cam said as he handed Tom his phone number.

"Ok, but heed my warning, as I said, I'm not an easy man to convince. I'm sure that between now and midday tomorrow, my mind will be working overtime trying to establish what exactly is going on. I can't see why anybody from Goa couldn't contact me through the hotel or business channels. I respect that you are not disclosing information that should come from somebody else, but that in itself makes me a little suspicious. I'm sure you can understand that. At the moment, I know very little about you, Cam, but I am a man who trusts my instincts, my instinct is telling me to trust you even though you look and smell like you've slept rough all night. My instinct has only let me down once before," Tom said.

At that, Cam made his way into the hallway and put his boots on, they shook hands and he left, making his way down the driveway to the gate. He found it amusing that he was leaving with a little more dignity than he arrived with. The electric gates opened as he approached them, walking through them he looked at the site of the hole that he had hidden in, reminiscing almost. He made his way back to his trusted VW and began his journey back to The Nag's Head where Jasmina awaited his return.

During his journey he reflected on his meeting with Tom, he was pleased he had finally tracked him down, pleased that he had arranged a meeting and pleased that he didn't get arrested. He was concerned about Jasmina's reaction of not being involved in the process, also her reaction of being left in bed alone that morning.

He couldn't help seeing similarities between Jasmina and her father. They were both strong people, who were not afraid to speak their mind, and offer an opinion. However, they were both of character containing depth and humility, together with an openness that he couldn't help but admire and like.

Cam arrived back at The Nag's Head. It was well into the afternoon now and he was fully aware of how long she had been alone. He almost leapt from the car and ran into the pub, he was excited about seeing her. As he burst into the bar area, his heart sank, he saw Jasmina sat on her own, looking very sorry for herself, he was overcome with guilt. As he approached her, he could see she had been crying.

"What's the matter?" he asked.

"You, you fool. You're the matter," she replied with a tense voice.

"I've been waiting here on my own for hours, not knowing if you were dead or alive, if you had changed your mind about me and gone back to Lincolnshire, or anything. All this after you had told me that you loved me." she said.

"Jasmina, I do, I wouldn't say it if I didn't. I love you and never want to be without you," he said as he pulled Jasmina to her feet giving her the tightest cuddle she had ever had.

"I love you too, you fool, I love you too," she said, with a little tension still in her voice.

On hearing this, Cam began to cry, his eyes filled with tears. His body tremored, almost like a sob. He was so delighted that Jasmina felt the same way as he did. It had been so long since anybody had told Cam that they loved him, he knew, at last and for the first time in his life, where he truly belonged, it was with Jasmina.

Cam had felt for so long that his life was comparable to lying in a cold, dark room with the uncertainty of ever seeing light again. That very moment had changed his whole perspective on things, he now compared his life to lying on a golden beach, being warmed by the bright sun, whilst listening to the sound of gentle waves breaking on the shore. He didn't want to break his hold on Jasmina because he didn't want people to know he had shed a tear, however, Jasmina knew, she knew him, knew what made him tick, she could also feel his body quivering with emotion.

After what seemed like an age of holding each other, a cuddle that they both would never forget, they made their way to a quiet seating area. They ordered some drinks and let their emotions settle.

They sat holding hands, not speaking to each other, just smiling. Through their touch, they could feel the commitment, sincerity and love for each other, no words were needed. Their love for each other yet again showed it was all-consuming.

It was almost as though they had forgotten the reason that had brought them to that place.

"Where have you been? What have you done?" Jasmina said.

"I'm afraid you may not agree with what I have done, please forgive me if you don't, but at the time it seemed the most instinctive thing to do," he said.

Jasmina looked at Cam with great concern.

"I met Thomas Allan. Initially he was going to have me arrested, that was until I mentioned Miss Singh. His whole demeanour then changed from one of hostility to one of calmness and curiosity. I explained that someone was here from Goa who wanted to meet him, I didn't mention names or yourself. He is definitely the man in the photo that you showed me. He is a man who is tough and gentle. I have arranged for us to meet him tomorrow at midday in a pub. I'm not sure if he will turn up or not. He has an amount of suspicion that I am possibly trying to do something underhanded. He kept saying that he is a hard man to convince, I suppose he means about me being honest. I hope I've done the right thing, my love," Cam said.

After a few seconds digesting what she had just heard, Jasmina looked at Cam and smiled.

"Firstly, Cam, I am so very grateful for everything that you do for me. I know that you love me and you would only do what you thought was right for me, so if it feels right for you, then it is right for me. This journey has brought our souls together, as every second passes, our souls become more and more entwined, never to be parted. I feel you, when I'm with you and when we're apart, I feel you deep inside my heart. I know you feel the same thing, if you didn't my heart wouldn't give itself to you.

Secondly, if it transpires that my father doesn't turn up and he wants nothing to do with me, there's nothing else I can do. If I'm honest that's what I expect to happen, if he doesn't show, then he is not worthy of the knowledge that, not only did my mother love him for the rest of her life, but also that he has a daughter.

It's enough that I have you, all I need is you," Jasmina explained.

Cam felt like he was floating on a cloud of love. For the rest of that day they emerged themselves in each other and as Jasmina had said, with their souls becoming forever entwined.

CHAPTER 10 THE DISCLOSURE

The following morning when Cam woke, he saw he'd been lying in a foetal position, with Jasmina's bottom pressed firmly in his lap. Her body against his and the smell of her sweet perfume made him feel as though he was luckiest man alive. He lay there trawling through some of his life's memories, wondering how he ever became so lucky. Was it always his destiny or was it just plain old luck? He couldn't answer those questions, what he could accurately assess was the way in which he had started to believe he was actually an 'ok' human being. He recollected all the false and malicious things that had been said about him during the breakdown of his marriage, not only to adults but also to his children. These things angered him immensely, and probably would do for the rest of his life.

Jasmina filled his heart with joy and love, but he knew that it was a different type of love to that which you give to, and receive from, your children. In relation to that love, he had a huge void. The opportunity to show and give love to his children had been cruelly taken from him after his divorce. Untruths had been told to his children which had created a division between him and them. He was left with a dilemma, did he tell his children the truth and risk alienating them further in addition to the potential of creating a division between his children and their mother? Or did he say nothing and wait in hope that his children see the truth for themselves over time? The latter option is what he was trying to do.

Jasmina stirred and immediately grabbed his arm, then gave a sigh of relief.

"You're still here," she mumbled in a sleepy voice.

She was obviously referring to the previous morning, when Cam had left her alone in the bed. He snuggled right up to her, with his head next to hers.

"I love you," he whispered in her ear.

She rolled to face him giving him a smile that, if it was the last thing he ever saw before he died, would ensure he died a happy man. He called them, 'her smiles'.

"Before we start this busy, important day, there's something that I would like you to know. We have no secrets, but I don't think I've told you this before," he started.

Jasmina looked at him softly and gave him her full attention.

"During the years I was married, some things happened that I'm not particularly proud of, nothing too dramatic, but it leaves you wondering why those things happened, and why you felt the way you did. You end up feeling guilty about everything. You live in a prison inside your head from where there is no escape.

Since meeting you, I have discovered that I am allowed to feel sensitivity, to feel intensity, I am allowed to breathe and look forward. I have never felt this way before, that's down to you. I have been set free. It's almost as though I have been exonerated from feeling the way I did. You have given me life, Jasmina, you have given me life."

"You too have given me life, we can now live that life together," she replied.

After wallowing in their love for each other, they eventually dragged themselves out of bed, got showered, dressed and fed in readiness for the day that lay ahead. Cam was slightly optimistic that Tom would turn up, Jasmina was not. Prior to going to bed, she had convinced herself that Thomas Allan would not be interested in seeing her, she did this as her defence mechanism to disappointment, it enabled her to relax a little and get some sleep. The morning brought fresh emotions, she felt tense, pessimistic and confused. It was understandable, after all, it was this moment, this one moment, that had caused her to travel thousands of miles, leave Goa for the first time in her life, spend every penny that she had, risk being arrested for using somebody else's passport, have her room burgled, be chased down the street, all to meet a man that didn't even know she existed.

They placed their bags into Cam's trusted VW and took one last look at The Nag's Head before setting off to The Pheasant. The Nag's Head would always be remembered affectionately by them. It had been their base for a couple of nights and whilst staying there they had, not only made significant steps towards achieving Jasmina's objectives, but also confirmed their love for each other. It was about an hour's journey. To say the journey was a tense one was an understatement. No more than a dozen words were spoken. Cam deliberately let Jasmina be alone with her thoughts, he realised that the next few hours could determine, not only what she did, but also how she felt, for the rest of her life. He also knew that the first few words, regarding how they were spoken, could determine the outcome of their meeting. His heart was crying for Jasmina, he knew he couldn't show it, it's not what she needed right now, she needed him to be strong and practical because she was in no state to be either.

They reached The Pheasant pub and subsequently parked on the rear car park. Thomas Allan's Range Rover was nowhere in sight. Cam knew this was a good thing, it would allow Jasmina enough time to get in the pub and settled before he arrived. Before exiting the car, Cam looked at Jasmina and took hold of her hand, desperately trying to reassure her.

"No matter what happens in there, just know that I love you," he said to her with deep affection.

"I know," she replied with a knowing smile on her face.

During the short walk to the pub, Jasmina gripped tightly onto Cam's arm, it was as though her legs were reluctant to work, her body was stiff, and she shivered uncontrollably.

Once inside the lounge area to the pub, Cam looked for a seat as near to the open fire as possible. He knew the heat would calm and settle Jasmina. The Pheasant was an old country pub, the type that would look completely at home either on a Christmas card or postcard, it encapsulated all the positive things about the English tradition of country pubs and ale. Cam fetched the drinks and Jasmina got settled, removing her coat. Cam leant towards Jasmina and whispered in her ear.

"I won't be sat next to you, but I will be with you."

A few minutes of being sat in silence passed, and then the pub door opened. Thomas Allan entered, wearing a long, black, formal-looking overcoat and grey suit trousers with black brogues. He gave the impression of being dressed for an important business meeting. He, again, wore a very stern look on his face, almost as though he was going into battle. He spotted Cam and made his way towards him. Cam was relieved that Thomas Allan had turned up, however, he felt apprehensive for Jasmina. He sensed that the reality of meeting her father had drastically uneased her.

"Hello, Tom," Cam said.

"Hello, Cam," Tom replied, as they shook hands.

"This young lady is the person who has come all the way from Goa to see you," Cam said whilst directing his open hand towards Jasmina.

"Hello, young lady," Tom said.

He did not offer a handshake, it was easy to see that, by his demeanour, he was very suspicious and defensive.

"If you need me I'll be in the bar area, I'll leave you two to talk," Cam said as he gave Jasmina a comforting smile and a kiss on the cheek.

Cam left the pub lounge, an awkward silence fell upon Jasmina and Thomas Allan which lasted for a couple of minutes. During this time, Jasmina looked into the log fire, not only did she get lost in its flickering flames, she felt the heat from it comforted her like a blanket tightly wrapped around her. It reminded her of Cam's log burner, just what she needed at that moment in time. Neither she nor Tom knew whether to start the conversation or not.

"Ok, young lady, I haven't got all day, I have things to do. Just tell me what you want me to know and I'll be on my way," Tom said in a forceful manner.

"It's about Sunita Singh," Jasmina said nervously.

"Yes I know, well what about her? Is she ok?" asked Tom.

"Well, I think there's something that she wanted you to know. I've come all this way to tell you in person because I thought it was the right thing to do," Jasmina said.

Tom was shocked that there could be anything Sunita would want him to know. He thought for a while, not knowing what to expect. Due to what had happened in Goa thirty-odd years ago, Tom became a little more defensive.

"Young lady, I don't know what it is that you want from me, whatever it is, please just tell me, I'm not prepared to sit in this pub all day," he said.

"Mr Allan, please be assured that I do not want anything from you. I am actually here to give you something, not to ask for something," Jasmina stated in a self-assured manner. She became slightly aggravated by Tom's attitude.

By this time, Jasmina had found the confidence to look him in the face. She, as Cam did, could tell that Thomas Allan was indeed the man in the photo. She could see why her mother felt attracted to him. Although appearing stern, she could see that he had an honest, no nonsense personality that was to be admired.

"I'm here to tell you some sad news I'm afraid. Sunita Singh passed away a few weeks ago," Jasmina said.

On saying this, Tom could see that her eyes filled with tears, his immediate reaction was to lean forward and offer his support.

"Young lady, I can see you're upset, I'm so sorry for your loss, did you know her well?" Tom asked.

He gradually sat back in his chair, it was his turn to look into the fire. Jasmina could see the devastation on his face, his stern look had turned into a look of complete sadness and shock. It was clear to see that the news was a massive blow to him. After a few minutes he stood up.

"Where are you going?" she asked, thinking that he was about to leave.

"I need a drink," he replied.

Tom made his way to the bar, he did need a drink but he also didn't want Jasmina to see how upset he really was, after all, what right did he have to be as upset as her, he thought?

Tom returned to Jasmina with two large glasses of brandy.

"I don't know if you need this, I certainly do," he said.

"How did you know Sunita?" asked Jasmina.

This was Jasmina's test to see how he would react, his reaction would be the answer to her question, as to whether to tell or not. If he tried to deny knowledge of Sunita, he would never gain the knowledge of his unknown daughter, if he acknowledged his relationship with her, then he would be presented with the information.

"I probably have no right to be upset over her death as I haven't seen her for thirty-odd years. I went to Goa on a business trip with my father, I was a lot younger then, indeed a young man. As I have no idea who you are, I won't go into detail, but Sunita and I became very close. Whenever we could we would meet and go off together, doing wonderful things. She was an amazing woman and taught me a lot about life. I have never forgotten her," he said.

Whilst speaking, Tom stared at the fire. Jasmina could see the tears in his eyes, she knew that he had taken himself right back to the days he spent with her mother in Goa. She could see that a warm depth had overtaken Tom, just like Cam had said, the mention of her mother's name transformed his whole demeanour. This was the sign that Jasmina needed. She was now sure that she would disclose who she was. She was still unsure of when, and how it would be done. She just knew her instinct would tell her.

"It's a long way to travel to inform me of that news, young lady. I'm sorry but I can't see what's in it for you," Tom said with an air of suspicion in his voice.

"For that reason alone it would be a long way to travel, yes, but still worth it. However, I also have another valid reason," Jasmina said.

"It would still need to be a good reason," Tom said.

"I have found my father. Until a few weeks ago I didn't know anything about him at all. I didn't even know he existed. I never needed to know because my mother was enough, but I believe it was her last wish that I should find him and inform him of my existence. Thomas Allan, you are my father," Jasmina disclosed.

On hearing this Tom had a complete look of disbelief, the stern look had returned to his face.

"Young lady, I don't know you, but is this a game?" he asked. "You come all this way, allegedly, to break some very sad news to me, and when I am deeply upset and vulnerable, you move in for the kill. I told your friend, Cam, that I am nobody's fool and will not be scammed. What do you want? Who are you?" Tom asked in a loud, angry voice.

Jasmina could see the upset and vulnerability in Tom, he still had tears in his eyes from the news of Sunita's death.

"Well, who are you?" he asked again whilst slamming his hand on the table.

"My name is Jasmina," she said.

On hearing this Tom went pale, almost as though somebody had just drained all the blood from his body, he slumped into his chair and just stared into Jasmina's eyes, and she into his.

It seemed like an age had passed when the stare eventually broke, caused by Cam entering the lounge after hearing the bang on the table. Jasmina beckoned Cam to sit by her and Tom.

"I now know it's true, it's true," Tom said.

"How do you know? Why the sudden change of heart?" she asked.

Still looking shell shocked, and with tears in his eyes Tom explained.

"Sunita, your mother, and me used to walk, talk and look at the stars a lot during the evenings. Our favourite place was a little garden on the outskirts of the hotel grounds, where it was beautiful, quiet, and the smell, it was intoxicating. We just used to lie on the ground, looking at the stars, making our plans together. We used to laugh at all the potential difficult situations that we would face, and how we would deal with them. It was like being in heaven on earth. Just me, Sunita and the stars. That was all we needed, nothing else. We even discussed the names of our children, we decided we would have four or five, after we were married, of course. The garden we laid in was the Jasmine garden. Named so, due to all the lovely flowers and the intoxicating, sweet smell. Hence we decided on the first name of our daughter, Jasmina, your name. After the first time we laid in that garden, I never wanted to forget that smell, I bought your mother some perfume to wear, it smelt of Jasmine, the exact same perfume you are wearing now. I would recognise it anywhere. I haven't smelt it since I was at the Hotel Jasmin. I loved your mother very, very much, so much so, that I haven't truly loved another woman since."

By now, Cam, Jasmina and Tom all had tears rolling down their cheeks and were highly emotional.

"If you loved each other so much, why didn't you get married to her and not dump her?" asked Jasmina.

"I didn't finish with your mother, my dear, she did me. On our last night, before I was due to fly home, we had arranged to meet but she didn't turn up. I was heartbroken, my natural instinct was to think that she had finished with me, either because I wasn't good enough for her because she was such a beautiful woman, or because she didn't want to move to England. But I would have moved to Goa, she knew that," he said.

"Tom, she didn't finish with you. She had to work extra hours, so she couldn't meet you, and because you didn't get in touch she assumed you had dumped her." Jasmina explained.

Tom began to sob, knowing that his chance of being happy with Sunita had ended due to a stupid misunderstanding.

"What a fool, what a stupid fool I was. I wasn't a very confident young man and your mother was the first girlfriend I ever had, I always thought she was too good for me," Tom stated.

"My instinct told me to ask her to marry me before I left Goa but I thought it might have been too soon for her and I didn't. I thought my instinct had let me down but it didn't. I should have asked her, I was right. What a fool I am, what a fool!!" he added.

"She never married. She loved you until the day she died, that I know. It was just before she died that she gave me the slightest inkling of who my father was, is," Jasmina said.

"All these years, all the times I have thought of, and longed to be with your mother, and I could have, and I could have known you. What a fool," Tom said.

Tom began to look even more sad and frustrated. It was clear that the recent revelations had a huge impact on him.

"I knew all those years ago that she was 'the one'. I still know that now. That's why I was so hurt when she didn't show up on that last night. I have missed her every single day of my life," Tom said.

Having almost forgotten about it, Jasmina produced the photo of her mother and father. Tom stared at it as though he had seen a ghost, it immediately transported him back to the time and place, the emotion on his face consisted of pleasure and pain.

"That was the only photo we ever had taken, it was long before the days of digital phone cameras, I remember it being taken, it was by your mother's sister. She was a lovely woman, very kind but strong, just like your mother, I think her name was Rupinder, although I could be wrong, it was a long time ago and my memories are full of your mother. Just look at your mother, she was so beautiful, not just physically but as a human being too. She was just perfect. If mobile phones had been invented then, your mother could have sent me a quick text and our whole lives could have been very different, complete perhaps," Tom explained as he stared lovingly at the photograph.

"Please may I have a copy?" he asked.

"Of course you can," Jasmina replied.

Jasmina stood up and declared that she needed use of a toilet. Tom too stood up to let her out of the corner in which she was sat, as she walked past Tom she felt a pair of arms hold her tight. It was Tom, he had not planned to, but felt compelled to, give Jasmina a hug. After her initial shock, and upon feeling the warmth and emotion from Tom, she reciprocated the embrace by throwing her arms around her father, and holding him tight, as tight as her strength would let her. She felt wonderful. For the very first time in her life she felt the protective hug and love from her father, the feeling that can only be had from a father's embrace. Tom felt the love flow from his body to his daughter's. To him, it felt like the most natural feeling in the world. At this, they both became tearful again for the duration of the embrace, which lasted a couple of minutes.

For Jasmina, the whole trip would have been worth it just for the wonderful feeling she had during the embrace, she was well aware that the first embrace and the emotion of it could never be repeated. Jasmina continued her journey to the toilets, giving Cam and Tom a chance to get to know each other, now that the awkwardness and tension had dissipated. They were unaware, but each of them had a healthy respect for the other.

Tom respected Cam due to his endeavour to do the very best for his, newly found, daughter. He admired the honesty, respect and determination that he had shown on their first meeting. Cam respected Tom due to his openness, humility and honesty, upon hearing the life-changing news he had just heard.

Cam informed Tom of the events Jasmina had encountered since leaving Goa, and how they had fallen in love. Tom could see the similarities between Cam and Jasmina, and himself and Sunita. Tom now identified the same personality traits in Jasmina that he had seen in Sunita. He now understood what drove Jasmina to deliver the sad news regarding her mother's death personally, it was loyalty.

Jasmina returned to the table and sat in the seat that she had vacated some minutes earlier. She looked at Tom in a somewhat serious manner.

"I'm thirty-four years old, there isn't much that I want in life now. I have found my father, who up until a few weeks ago, I didn't know existed. I have found the love of my life in Cam, he definitely is the one for me, and I have no intentions of ever being without him. The only thing that I could ever wish for to make my life more perfect, but it can't happen, would be that my mother, your 'one', was here to share this moment. I now know that the only thing that could have made her life even more perfect, would be to have spent it with you, her 'one'. I know I would like to, and it would help to keep the happy memories alive of your time with her, could I call you father?" Jasmina asked.

Tom's eyes, once again, began to fill with tears. "Jasmina, those weeks your mother and I had together were, undoubtedly, the happiest days of my life. I feel it a privilege to have known your mother. Again, I would feel it a privilege if you wanted to call me your father, although I don't feel as though I deserve such an honour. I know that if you do, every time you say it, and every time I hear it, your mother will be in our thoughts," Tom replied.

Tom held his hands out to Jasmina, who duly placed hers within them, they looked into each other's eyes, and for the first time in her life she addressed someone in such a manner.

"Father," she simply said.

"Daughter," he said.

"I never thought I would ever say that word to my own child, daughter," he said.

"I thought Laura was your daughter?" Jasmina said.

"She is my stepdaughter, her mother and I married when she was five years old. Her mother and I didn't really get on, the first few years weren't too bad, but after that it was a living hell. It didn't help when I told her of my relationship with Sunita, although it was nothing to do with her, she and Laura had a right go at me, their true colours shone through that day. Perhaps she could feel that my heart was elsewhere. She left me for a much younger man some years ago, he was her personal trainer. I don't know what happened to her but I'm sure he was only after money, she took enough from me to keep her and him happy for some time. I've lived with Laura since, she didn't want to go with her mother, I think she's had it far too comfortable and easy living with me. I tend not to argue with her anymore because the stress - it upsets me too much. I sometimes think she is a machine," Tom said.

"Yes, that's the impression I got of Laura when I met her," Cam said.

"Unfortunately, due to her upbringing, before moving in with me, money was tight for her and her mother. Now it seems that is all that drives her, I think she feels the need to show the world that she isn't poor anymore. She has a controlling nature caused by a deep insecurity, it's almost like it completely takes over her, she likes to control people and things around her. I think her mother and me somehow, without intention, created a monster who certainly is her mother's daughter. She thought that she would get accepted more easily in business if she changed her name to Laura, she was actually christened Shasney. She seems to think that her name will earn her more respect than hard work and business acumen, she is wrong. The reason I retired was so as not to have to be in her company any longer than I had to. Money, the problem with money is that it attracts all the wrong people to you, they think it's all about prestige, glitz and glamour, but when the money goes, they go. They don't realise that money changes people, it changes perspective, they forget what's really important and just focus on wealth. It's as though it drains the goodness out of some people. That's what made your mother so special, she was not interested in money, only love. All we ever needed was love and each other. I would give every penny I've had and ever will have just to have an opportunity to tell her that I never stopped loving her," Tom said.

"Some things are grown in the heart, and they never die. I'm sure she knew," Jasmina said.

The afternoon in the pub passed quickly, it was full of conversation, lots of drinks (mainly non-alcoholic due to them having to drive) and the three of them getting to know each other. Even during those few hours, Jasmina and her father had developed a bond and a genuine fondness of each other.

Cam was delighted for them both, and to have witnessed this take place.

Upon leaving the pub, with addresses and phone numbers exchanged, they agreed to meet again in the very near future.

"Father, you are a wonderful man, I am very pleased to have found you and I'm very proud to be your daughter," Jasmina said as she kissed her father on the cheek.

"No, Jasmina, I truly am the lucky one. I know how proud your mother would have been of you whilst watching you grow into this, this beautiful woman," he replied.

They said their goodbyes and made their journeys to their respective homes.

Over the next few weeks, Jasmina and Tom spoke many times on the phone, they met up with him in Surrey and he visited them at Cam's bungalow. He liked it there very much, so much that he stayed over for a couple of nights. The warmth and homeliness he felt there were the complete opposite feelings to what he had at his home in Surrey. Sleeping on the settee, listening to, and watching the log burner slowly fade, gave him the opportunity to be alone with his thoughts, far away from the dog-eat-dog world of business and money. It also gave him a reason to be away from the controlling environment created by Laura. He understood the peace and tranquility that the bungalow offered Jasmina and Cam.

Since gaining the knowledge that Sunita loved him until the day she died, and now actually having his own daughter, it gave him many things to think about and decisions to make. He could feel a transformation taking place in him, reverting from a lonely man who had deliberately shunned any form of relationship in a bid to protect himself, to the person he used to be, open hearted. He knew of the dangers of being hurt, but also the benefits of giving his love to, and feeling the love from his daughter, more than compensated for any risk. For the first time in thirty-odd years, he knew he was living a full life, embracing all the good that it brings, together with all the not so good. It was good for him to be living a life, whilst with Jasmina and Cam in Lincolnshire, that wasn't dominated by money or wealth, but by love that together with its realisation and acceptance, brings the deeper joy that wealth never could.

He had informed Laura of Jasmina's existence, the news wasn't accepted with love and appreciation, but Tom knew, that was always going to be the case. Laura's goal in life was not family and love, but money and power. Cam and Jasmina never mentioned their suspicions regarding Laura because they didn't want to create any more stress for Tom, or accuse an innocent person of something where there was no proof.

Jasmina had set the wheels in motion regarding obtaining her own passport and had legalised her stay in the UK.

In an attempt to try and bring his family together Tom had arranged a meal in The Allan Hotel. As Christmas was approaching he thought it would be a good idea to combine the two, he had selected that venue so that his guests could stay the night in the hotel, without worrying about travel and transport. His guest list included, Jasmina, Cam, Laura and Jasmina's aunt, Rupinder. Tom had contacted her through the Hotel Jasmin, paid for her flights and arranged for her to have time off from work. He hoped it would be a lovely surprise for Jasmina, she hadn't been back to Goa since first leaving. He truly hoped it would develop into a night that would never be forgotten.

CHAPTER 11 THE UNITED FAMILY

A week before Christmas the big day had arrived, the day the family got to know each other and became a true family, it was almost as though Jasmina and Tom had waited their whole lives for this day. For them, the only thing that could have made it more perfect was if Sunita had been there in person, without doubt she was there in spirit, and of course, people's hearts. This get-together, gathering, party, celebration was only taking place because of her existence and the wonderful person she was, it could be said it was taking place in her honour.

At this time of year London was like most other cities, frantic with activity. The traffic was nose to tail for what appeared to be twenty-four hours a day, the pavements were crowded for what appeared to be the same amount of time, and the noise, it never stopped. The city was lit up, not only by the usual street and shop lighting but also by Christmas decorations, both inside and outside of nearly every building. The effect this had on people was evident to see, they were clearly excited and saying "hello" to each other, even though they had never met before, or even if they had passed each other on the same street a thousand times before without acknowledgement. The goodwill was flowing in abundance. Cam and Jasmina looked out from their hotel window and witnessed these events.

"This is exactly how people should behave every single day," Cam said with a warm smile on his face.

"Yes it is, my love, but we are wise enough to know it won't last," Jasmina replied with an air of truth and sadness.

The hotel room they were staying in, courtesy of her father, was magnificent. Neither one of them had stayed in anything so plush and luxurious before and they were appreciative of her father's efforts to make them comfortable and feel loved. However, during the week prior, they had seen a different side to city life, they had been working with a charity and feeding the homeless from a soup kitchen. Both enjoyed their participation in that, not because they thought they were changing somebody's life but because for a few minutes whilst the homeless person, firstly smiled on receipt of the food, and secondly sat enjoying it, was happy. That moment potentially being the catalyst for that person to change, or at least seek help to change their life.

The luxury room made them feel guilty about the homeless, but they couldn't possibly upset Tom by insisting on staying elsewhere.

Cam didn't actually own any smart trousers, he made sure he had clean jeans, shirt and shoes and hoped he wouldn't embarrass Jasmina too much. He had never been a lover of wearing suits or had put too much emphasis on his appearance at such functions. Smart casual was the best he could usually offer.

Jasmina, on the other hand, was wearing a new dress that was befitting of the occasion. Cam insisted on buying it for her, he wanted her night to be perfect and everything that she wanted it to be. It was a black sleeveless/backless full length evening gown that hugged her figure, and was covered in sequins. Her jewellery included items of her mother's, a simple gold necklace that was the perfect length to hang at the front of her dress and just above her cleavage. One bracelet was made of gold and patterned like a snake wrapping itself around her wrist, her other bracelet was made from string and multi-coloured beads, it was one that Jasmina had made for her mother when she was a child, and one that her mother never removed from her wrist. Jasmina wanted to do the same, live her life without it being removed. Her shoes were a little less glamorous, they were black leather, no pattern, with small heels. Jasmina in some ways was very much like Cam, putting practicality first.

Cam stared at Jasmina.

"You are the most beautiful thing I have ever seen," he said, whilst staring at her adoringly.

"Thank you, my love," she replied, returning the look of adoration.

"Before tonight starts in earnest, I want you to know how very proud of you I am, and that you make me feel like the luckiest, happiest man alive. Every second of my life that I spend with you is one that I treasure. Now that we are together, everything I see looks better, everything I touch feels better, everything I smell smells better and everything I feel feels better. It is all down to you, my love, my one and only love," Cam said.

He held Jasmina in his arms and kissed her neck. He smelt her sweet, Jasmine-scented perfume, the very same one that her mother used to wear, he held her like he never wanted to let her go. They could again feel each other's heartbeat and the intensity of their love.

"Shall we give the party a miss and stay here?" he asked jestfully whilst looking at the bed.

"Don't be silly, we have the rest of our lives to stay in bed together," she replied whilst slapping him on the arm.

They put on their respective jacket and shoulder cape and left the room to meet with the other guests.

In the foyer area they met with the other guests, apart from Rupy, she was waiting on a signal from Tom as when to arrive. Everyone was greeting everyone else. It was the first time Cam and Jasmina had been officially introduced to Laura. Laura was very polite to them, spoke at the correct times and smiled at the correct times. Cam, being an observer of people, somehow thought it was all too manufactured, too perfect and flawless. Conversation flowed until Jasmina suddenly stopped talking and began to stare over the shoulder of Laura. It could possibly be perceived as being rude, until you knew the reason for her distraction. Jasmina's attention was drawn by a lady she knew, but never expected to see, let alone be in the same room as her, in the same city in the same country. It was her aunt.

"Aunt Rupy!" Jasmina said in a loud, excited manner.

She ran to Rupy and upon reaching her she gave her the most almighty hug. The pair of them hugged each other as though they hadn't seen each other for years, not weeks. It was easy to forget that they had, very recently, lost a woman they both very much loved.

"How? Why? When?" Jasmina asked Rupy, astonished.

Rupy just looked at Tom. At that moment Jasmina's love for her father deepened. She knew he had done this for her and Rupy, somewhat taking the spotlight off himself. She knew that's what good fathers do, and expect nothing in return, the things that can't be seen. She rushed over to her father.

"Thank you. You're the best father any daughter could ever wish for," she said.

Tom became emotional yet again, his eyes filled with tears and his heart filled with pride. He wanted to tell Jasmina that she was the best daughter a father could wish for but he couldn't, Laura was within earshot, and he didn't want to upset her any more than he potentially had done already. He knew that the recent events would have an effect on her but didn't know, or couldn't assess, to what extent because she was a hard person to read. This highlighted the fact that it was the unseen things a person does, the deeds that are unquantifiable and cannot be measured, that makes them the good people that they are.

Everybody was ready to start celebrating, they were all dressed in their finest attire, Cam being the exception, and all in exceptional good spirit.

They were dining across the road at a restaurant that was owned by a friend of Tom's. He often dined there often because he didn't like to put extra pressure on his staff by them trying to impress him, or the faffing that they do whilst trying to impress him.

They entered the restaurant and were shown to their table, it was undoubtedly the best table in the house and slightly elevated, giving a view across the entire restaurant. All of his guests were suitably impressed. The atmosphere in the restaurant was electric, everyone had a smile on their face and was intent of having a good time. It wasn't particularly Cam's choice of venue but he was gracious enough to participate in the celebratory atmosphere and not detract from it.

He could see that everyone was doing their very best to make Rupy feel at home and at ease, it appeared to be working. She was very engaging and displaying in abundance, that beautiful character trait of humility. He could see by her personality, that she too would have preferred something a little less ostentatious, but she was wholeheartedly embracing the occasion. Cam looked at Tom and saw a man sat there looking like he had just won the lottery, and of course he had, not just by having a daughter such as Jasmina, but also by gaining this opportunity to live forever in the bosom of his family. He could see that he appeared to be revelling in his new role of being a father to Jasmina.

Cam's attention then moved to Laura, again he thought that she was a difficult person to assess. He observed that her manners were perfect, that she said lots of words but actually said nothing, and smiled without emotion, the perfect credentials for a businesswoman, he concluded. His attention then moved to Jasmina, he could see that she was glowing with pride, self-confidence and optimism. He was thrilled that she appeared to be having a wonderful time after her recent troubles.

During the food courses, the drinks, conversation and good will flowed. Cam continued with his people observations and noticed that Laura, still saying the right things at the right times, and smiling at the right times was doing some assessing of her own. When smiling in conversation, she lacked any joy in her eyes, he empathised with her somewhat as she had just discovered the existence of her half-sister. Her life too was dramatically changing due to events that were far beyond her control.

As the guests became more inebriated, their inhibitions lowered, this is always a good recipe for laughter, Cam thought. He wasn't wrong, the more the guests laughed, the more it became contagious. They were giving away secrets and opinions that normally would never be made public, but now they all had a bond, they were family. The quality of the food was excellent, during every course, the plates were cleaned, without a crumb being wasted. They all thought it was a feast fit for kings. The empty plates and dishes from the sweet course had been taken away and the guests were awaiting their coffee order. Cam, who was always polite and considerate towards others and their feelings, knew that this was the perfect time. He didn't know if the appropriate time would arise, and if it hadn't he would not have forced the issue, but in his heart of hearts he knew this was the moment.

He stood up from his seat, not wishing to attract attention to himself, and slowly walked unnoticed the few steps to where Jasmina was sat. Everybody was engaging in conversation and laughter, but when the time was right, he deliberately cleared his throat. The table went quiet, at this Cam knelt down on one knee and looked deep into Jasmina's eyes.

"My darling, Jasmina, you are the most special, gifted, strong, loving and caring woman that I have ever met. You inspire me, you thrill me and you fill me with love. You have shown me that a beautiful woman can be just as beautiful on the inside. The humility that you show towards others is felt and admired by anybody who has had the great pleasure of knowing you. I thought my life was good, complete, and nothing was lacking, that is until I met you. How wrong I was. My heart is now full and my eyes have been opened to how life can be lived, full of love and joy. There is not one second of any day that I want to be without you, I want to spend the rest of my life with you as man and wife," Cam said before a silenced table with a slight tremble in his voice.

He then pulled from his pocket a small ring box, and opened it whilst presenting it to Jasmina.

"Jasmina, if it is acceptable to your father, will you marry me?" he asked.

By this time, the whole of the restaurant had fallen silent and were absorbed by Cam and Jasmina. The atmosphere was now full of anticipation and expectancy.

Jasmina looked at her father, who looked shocked, bewildered and proud. With tears in his eyes and a smile on his face that could light up the world, and being unable to speak due to the emotion, he nodded continuously in a most agreeable manner. Jasmina looked at Aunt Rupy with a look of complete surprise, she looked back at her with a look of joy, contentment and pride, although she didn't need any help with her decision, she knew that Aunt Rupy was thrilled with the idea of her becoming Cam's wife.

Jasmina turned and looked at Cam, her eyes staring straight into his. She replied in the sincerest, softest voice,

"Yes."

Cam placed the engagement ring on her petite and delicate finger, and on seeing this, the whole restaurant stood up and cheered. The atmosphere became euphoric, there were people clapping, crying and screaming. Amongst the frenzied celebrations, Cam embraced Jasmina, and for the those few seconds they managed to close the world outside, just focusing on each other. They both knew that they were going to be blissfully happy, spending the rest of their lives together.

"Champagne for everyone!" Tom shouted.

"What are you doing?" Laura asked Tom.

"It's pointless having money and being miserable, I've worked hard all my life and I'm going to spend it how I like. We're celebrating!!!" Tom replied.

The champagne flowed, the volume of the music increased, the party had started. The whole restaurant, drank, danced and partied until the early hours. Everyone in the restaurant congratulated them and looked at Jasmina's engagement ring at some point during the evening. It was as though their personal happiness had increased everyone else's, a once in a lifetime magical moment.

Jasmina's engagement ring was made from gold, with a gold claw holding a single diamond. It was relatively small and unobtrusive. When purchasing it, Cam wanted it to reflect Jasmina, beautiful and petite.

Laura was the first of Tom's guests to leave, giving the reason that she didn't want to be late for work in the morning, albeit a Sunday. She wished Cam and Jasmina well, although Cam was still not convinced about her sincerity.

Shortly after, Cam, Jasmina, Tom and Rupy all left the restaurant together. As they stepped onto the pavement outside, they all immediately felt the cold night air. Christmas lights were still shining bright from all directions, giving the effect of them being in a winter wonderland. Just prior to crossing the road to go back to the hotel, Jasmina, who was in front of Cam with her father, looked behind and gave him one of those smiles again, the one that reminded him of being the luckiest man in the world. Rupy, who was stood next to Cam, looked at him with a knowing smile on her own face. They were all feeling wonderfully happy, warm inside and full of love. A perfect moment in time.

Jasmina, holding onto Tom's arm, stepped into the road with him, followed by Cam and Rupy, who was holding onto his arm. Cam heard an engine start and rev hard, his career had made him alert to such sounds. He remembered the stolen 'hot hatches' back in the 1990s that were dangerously raced around the streets by joyriders. Cam looked to his right and saw Laura in her white Audi accelerating hard towards them. Instinctively, he knew she wasn't going to stop, she was heading straight for Jasmina and Tom, without hesitation he flung Rupy to the side and, without consideration for his own safety, dived towards Jasmina and Tom. The Audi was travelling so fast he only had time to push one person out of the way of the ever nearing machine. On reaching Jasmina he gave her the most almighty shove, she was unaware that it was coming and flew to the other side of the road, landing in a heap on the pavement. Due to its speed, the Audi collided with both Cam and Tom with tremendous force, bouncing them high into the air as though they were made from cardboard, the dull crunching sound of the impact on their bodies was a sound that Jasmina would never forget. Their distorted bodies landed more than thirty yards away from where the impact had taken place. The Audi continued to travel at speed for another fifty yards where it came to an abrupt halt after colliding with a lamp post. There was no movement from inside the car.

A stillness fell upon the scene, as though time had stood completely stopped. People appeared to freeze to the spot with no sound to be heard, hoping they were in a bad dream. However, it was not a dream.

Both Cam and Tom lay alone on the cold and damp tarmac, perfectly still amongst the eerie silence and festive lights.

Jasmina was in complete shock but she knew that the man who had just saved her life, who she loved so dearly and only a few hours earlier had agreed to marry, was dead.

She also knew that her newly found father was also dead.

No medical confirmation was needed, she could feel the pain in her heart, soul and in every cell of her body.

The most joyous, perfect evening that she could have ever imagined had somehow ended in such tragedy.

Two very bright candles in her life had gone out, forever.

CHAPTER 12 THE JASMINE GARDEN

On the 21st December the following year, a year to the day of the tragedy, Jasmina and Rupy were sat in the Jasmine garden of the Hotel Jasmin, Goa. It was a warm, beautiful and clear day, the sky was completely blue, and a gentle breeze blew as the sea glistened in the distance.

Jasmina and Rupy sat discussing that fateful evening and the events of the subsequent year. They never discovered fully why Laura had done what she had. They assumed it was either because of greed and the thought that Jasmina may somehow be involved in the business, or down to being insecure and not being able to control Tom the way she had done so for a number of years.

Tom, unbeknown to Jasmina, on gaining knowledge of her existence, had altered his will. His estate was to be split equally between Jasmina and Laura, with a clause that if one of them died before the other, the survivor would inherit everything. Unexpectedly, this is what happened to Jasmina, she now had more wealth than she knew what to do with. It was a situation that she never would have willingly put herself in.

She knew, deep down inside, that Cam would also have done what she wanted to do, share her good fortune and wealth with deserving people. She had started by giving all the employees at the Hotel Jasmin shares in it. She had separated the hotel from the rest of the group so that it could be run independently, thus providing staff with an influence on their own destiny and some ownership in what they were working for. She had employed managers to deal with the rest of the business, for the meantime anyway.

Jasmina had located Cam's children, she wanted them to know and never forget that their father was a wonderful, brave, loving and caring man. She discussed his funeral with them, as it was the last time they could ever decide anything to have influence on him. She also discussed his much loved bungalow, which she subsequently purchased from them. She needed to keep it, after all it was the place where they had discovered their love for each other, it held such beautiful memories for her, especially the blazing log burner. It was their place, their place of tranquility, the place where they could shut the world outside and just devote their time and love to each other. She wanted it to always remain as their place.

The bench on which they were sat had a brass plaque on its rear, which read:

In loving memory of a dearly missed and wonderful mother and grandmother, Sunita Singh.

In loving memory of a dearly missed and wonderful father, and grandfather, Thomas Allan.

In loving memory of a dearly missed and wonderful man and father, Cameron Grant.
'The One'.

Donated by Jasmina Singh and Maisie Singh.

Jasmina could feel a wet patch on her thigh, she looked down and saw that Colin had dribbled where he had been laying his head.

"Oh, Colin," she said as she gently moved his head. Colin in no great rush, slowly and reluctantly moved away and laid on the grass.

She had taken Colin to Goa so that he could spend the rest of his life in a warmer climate. It appeared to suit him. The hotel guests seemed to love him, and he them. The movement in his joints had improved greatly, in truth, Colin was another part of Cam that she didn't want to let go.

Next to Rupy and Jasmina, sat in her pram, was three-month-old, Maisie Singh. Unknown to Jasmina and Cam, that at the time of his tragic death, she was pregnant. Maisie was the reason she presently had no interest in business, she knew how valuable time was and didn't want to miss a second of her life.

Maisie was named after Cam's mother who had passed away some years before. If Maisie had been a boy, then he would have been called Richard after Cam's father who had also passed away some years before.

In Maisie, she could see a mixture of her father, mother and Cam. In her eyes she was truly a gift, the biggest gift of all, one that she never expected but welcomed with every cell of her being. Maisie had lots of dark hair, beautiful olive coloured skin and the biggest brownest eyes you could ever imagine. When she looked at people it was as though her eyes were searching their souls. She intended that Maisie spend time in Lincolnshire with her, this would let her learn about her father's existence, personality and hopefully his family. She didn't want Maisie to experience what she had, years of not knowing who her father was. Jasmina wanted Maisie to share in her brothers' and sisters' lives too, she was sure that she could bring some light into their lives, and that they could provide her with love and security, something that Laura failed to recognise, appreciate or give chance to.

"I think the time is right, Aunt Rupy," she said.

"So do I," Rupy replied.

Jasmina had three urns of ashes, her mother's, her father's, and Cam's.

She started to spread the combination of her parents' ashes onto the perfectly manicured lawn.

"This is where it all started for you two, holding hands, gazing at the stars, and falling in love with each other. Your life together back then was all too brief, now you can spend the rest of eternity together, gazing at the stars and staying in love. I love and miss you both," she said.

She then paused and reflected on the sadness of the lost time her parents had missed. She then started to spread Cam's ashes, this was hard for her, she knew, that once his ashes had left her hand and disappeared into the garden, that would be the last ever physical contact she would have with any part of him. She knew it was the right and proper thing to do, keeping his ashes in an urn would be like caging an eagle, a thing that flourished in its natural environment, needing nothing else other than to be left alone.

"My love, I have brought you here because I know it's a place that you have never been, and I knew you would like it. Whilst you rest here, Maisie and I promise to visit and speak with you as much as we can.

Whilst you rest and sleep at night, you now will always have the sweet smell of my perfume, Jasmine, surrounding you. Its scent intensifies in the evening, so that when you sleep you will know that I am with you. I love you, Cam."

After Jasmina had spread the ashes she knew that all three of them would be with her forever, in a place of beauty and tranquility. She knew that many of life's trials lay ahead, waiting to test her, but she was confident that the values that Cam and her parents had taught her, would enable her to cope, and if times got really tough, she had her Aunt Rupy to fall back on. She also knew that the three of them together would not only survive, but love and enjoy each other.

Jasmina had been tested, had suffered and had lost loved ones, but she remained optimistic, with a heart full of love and understanding, given to her by 'The One'.

17403714R00051

Printed in Great Britain
by Amazon